HeartsBlood

BOOK ONE

UnLife

1

As an out of work actor, I often find myself in shady situations.

Like sharing a three-bedroom condo with ten people I barely knew.

Or trying to sneak into said housing by climbing in through the balcony to avoid my live-in landlord from hell.

It was only one floor up, and an easy climb, thanks to conveniently placed brickwork. I'd first realized it could be a good way in and out when I watched one of my house mate's boyfriends doing a dash down there when her *other* boyfriend showed up unexpectedly.

That she had the time and energy for not one, but two—or possibly more—relationships, left me

a little jealous. But I didn't know much about her or how her life really was. Same with all my house mates. Our living conditions may have been close, but nothing else about our relationships were.

The sun was high, spreading yellow light over the scrubby, rocky hills. The sky-high palm tree casting a shadow over me had little cooling affect and sweat beaded over my pale skin.

With a final grunt, I rolled myself over the railing and came face to face with Lisa, squatting on the dusty sun lounge having a smoke.

She choked. "The fuck? Kitty?"

I cursed internally as well. So much for avoiding my landlord.

"Sorry, I left my keys in my room." I pointed through the dirty glass sliding door toward the tiny converted walk-in cupboard that I was lucky enough to not share with half a dozen others like the larger bedrooms. I kept moving, heading in that direction, hoping to pass by without incident.

Lisa shot to her feet and blocked my path. She was a tall thin redhead, with adorable freckles, and a tongue like a viper. She was also one hell of a guitarist and got an occasional big gig with whatever band she hadn't yet been kicked out of. The condo we all lived in had belonged to her grandparents, and she rented rooms out to struggling wannabes to make the rest of her ends meet. She really was

unlife

undeniably a bitch though. I think she enjoyed lording the fact she'd made something of a name for herself over those of us who hadn't.

I forced out an awkward chuckle and tried to side-step her, as though she wasn't obviously getting in my way on purpose.

She took a long drag, and her words came out smokey in my face. "You owe rent."

That, I knew. I was just hoping to avoid having to pay up for a little longer. I was overdue on a bunch of bills, and my bank account was like Mother Hubbard's cupboards. Bare. Pilot season had been a bust, and I was eking out the last of my pay from a shoddy car dealership commercial.

I sidled a little closer to the door. "Oh, sorry, slipped my mind! I'll get it to you soon."

"Today. And it'll be an extra fifty on top."

My mouth dropped and I froze with my fingers on the door handle. "What? Why?"

She flicked her cigarette butt over the balcony. Her eyes were narrowed by a sly smile. "Rent's gone up."

A million arguments and furies rattled around in my brain. I was already paying way too much for a space I could barely lay a sleeping bag down in. Lisa helped herself to my belongings as though anything in the building were hers. She even charged an "admin fee" on top of utilities share. The whole thing was a rort.

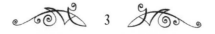

Her eyes narrowed further. "What's up, Kitty? You don't like it, you can leave. Can't say I've heard good things about the housing market at the moment though. And for someone with a credit rating like yours ..." She tilted her head and pouted, as though there was any sympathy in her venomous blood.

My shoulders sagged. My voice came out scratchy and too high. "I'll get the rent to you."

Somehow. If I could only pull magic money out of my ass.

I tugged the door open and skittered through, across the jumble of living room and three house mates lounging in there, then shut myself into my tiny, private space.

The screen on my phone had a nasty crack, but it still connected well enough to the neighbors Wi-Fi to avoid data charges. I sat on my sleeping bag, leaned against my suitcase-slash-wardrobe, and checked my emails, hoping for a miracle.

Scrolling through the spam, a subject line caught my eye.

Re: Casting for Downtime Dirtbags

Eyes wide, I held my breath and opened the email.

Thanks for auditioning, yadda yadda, great technical skills, missing the right emotional oomph, appreciate your time, not for us.

I groaned and thumped my head back against my suitcase. No miracle for me today.

unLife

It always seemed to be the excuse. I had put so much work and time into my acting skills, but I was always missing *something*.

I had blamed my agent, Harvey, at first, for the lack of roles coming my way. But lately I'd been trying to get out on my own to make things happen, and still, nothing. Maybe it was just me. *Maybe I don't have what it takes.*

I flicked through all the open tabs in my browser for casting calls and extra work, getting to the tab at the end. The Jenny Kurtz agency. My dream agent. That tab had been open since before I left home. Before I signed with Harvey instead, telling myself he was just my way to get started, until I'd proven myself in the industry enough to shoot for bigger goals.

If I had been brave enough to try for the Jenny Kurtz agency right away, would things have been different now? Could I still turn things around if I went to her? Would she even consider me?

I wouldn't ever know. I didn't have time to dream about becoming a star right now. I had to earn some quick cash so I didn't end up homeless.

There was only one thing for it.

I was going to have to go to Harvey and beg him for any job he had going, then beg even harder for an advance. I could already imagine the leer on his greasy mouth while he told me he had a hemorrhoid

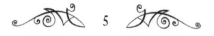

cream commercial or 'useless infomercial woman' role for me. *Ugh. I hate him so much.*

Harvey Hall was a second-rate agent to struggling actors. His one claim to fame was that he'd signed a few of the bigger names when they were still broke enough to hope that his representation would lead to a big role. I had no illusions about good old Harvey, and I'm sure he harbored no illusions about me either. As soon as I built a resume, I'd be leaving his ass in the dust without a single look back. Since he'd been too busy to answer my calls after signing on a whole new stable of girls fresh off the bus—girls willing to work naked or be billed as *Hooker Number Three*—me dreaming about better agents didn't feel unfair.

Harvey had been giving me the cold shoulder for a while now, so I stormed out to go to his office in person. The LA lunchtime crowd was hectic, sidewalks filled with people networking over food that I eyed jealously. I'd never afford half those meals.

If I ever do get rich and famous, I swear I'm going to be one of those stars that the paparazzi always catches coming out of some trendy restaurant. I love food in all of its forms, and I read menus like some people read travel brochures, making lists of the places I want to eat at when I have enough money to afford them. Good food for me was better than sex. Or at least was more easily available and with less attached baggage, which was far more preferable.

I moved fast, hoping to get to Harvey's while his secretary was on her lunch break. I arrived just as she was trotting out.

I lurked out of sight, waiting for her to leave, then dashed in. I felt a little ashamed that I let the cold, glasses wearing matron that guarded my agent's door scare me off, but the woman was truly frightening. I'd rather brave a dragon than her.

I appeared in a burst in front of Harvey's desk, wide-eyed as though I'd even startled myself at my daring appearance.

"Ah, Kitty, how nice of you to drop in." He managed to sound happy to see me even though his mouth twisted like he'd licked a lemon. Something of an actor himself. "What can I do for you?"

Deep breath. Ask for what you want. I stuttered, "I was hoping you could get me a job. My rent is due, my car actually needs gas to run, and while I could stand to lose a little weight, starvation is not a good thing." I bit my tongue on that last bit. I was giving him more ammunition to use against me. He'd been on my back to lose weight ever since I'd signed with him. I wasn't overweight, but I enjoyed my food, and sometimes I didn't make it to the gym as often as I could. "I just, really need something right away. Anything."

"Calm down, little lady. You're a keen one, aren't

you?" He steepled his sausage fat fingers together and said, "Actually, this is great timing. I may have something for you."

The smugness in his voice made my relief tentative. "What is it?"

"It's a Live Action Role Playing event," he said, "Not an on-screen acting job, but it's still acting, and it pays well."

I frowned. "Role playing?"

"I'm not talking about some kids fighting orcs in their backyard, this is real prestige stuff. A club downtown runs these vampire nights now and then. A bunch of guys who like to pretend they're bloodsuckers and chase pretty girls around. The club brings in a few willing victims, actresses hired to take part in the game. The girl who was supposed to do it got a lucky break and landed a nice role on a new series. Great for her, but she can't make it to the gig tonight and has left me high and dry. How about it, you want to play the victim?"

Are you kidding me? "You want me to play a game?" I stared at him. His greasy moon face was filmed with sweat despite the air conditioner's steady cooling blow. He stank of cheap cologne and cigar smoke, just like some slime ball out of a noir flick. I had to wonder how much of the shine was from sweat and how much of it was from the pomade trickling out of his thinning, slicked back hair.

unLife

I could see my own reflection in the gleaming surfaces of the awards hanging on his walls—a pale, oval face, dark hair, and a mouth that is perhaps a trifle too thin by some standards. I can't count the number of times I've been told I should get collagen injections. There was a little too much white showing around my eyes and a slight tremble in my chin. I looked scared, and I didn't like that at all. If I could see that fear so could Harvey, and Harvey is like a dog. Let him smell fear and he will move in for the kill. I could tell from the way he was watching me that he knew he had me.

He locked me in his gaze. "High end LARP events like this are easy money. Isn't that what you're after? You get these rich bastards willing to spend good money to play out their fantasies. Sometimes we get warlords from alternate universes who want to enslave a buxom wench, or wannabe Lords of Crazyshit Manor who want to duel at dawn and win the fair maiden, and so on. Lots of actors do it, not that they'll ever admit it. There's a non-disclosure agreement you have to sign, and you can't tell anyone because discretion matters to these folks. Are we clear?"

The mention of rich bastards and NDAs threw up red flags in my head. Wasn't there some rumor about some of Harvey's girls going on weird jobs and never coming back? Whether it was snuff films or some event that turned them off the industry for

good, no one knew. It was just conspiratorial gossip mostly. But I couldn't shake the shiver of doubt.

"Come on, Harvey. I've been in seven movies already, two of them as the lead. I know they were B-movies, but still … Surely you can find me something better than some weird game." I was pleading now. I doubted any real actors did this kind of gig. It sounded strictly amateur to me, and I was getting tired of being an amateur. But what other option did I have?

"Listen, Kitty, it isn't my fault." Harvey went all serious, leaning across his desk so far his puffy belly melted into the edges of it and rolled over the top. "Every casting director with a movie on their desk is looking for a cute blonde with a huge rack and a nice ass. Blonde is back in style, and you and your bookish goth chick look is played out. Not that I'm saying your rack isn't nice."

I wanted to smack the sleazy grin off his face, but just balled my fists at my sides where he couldn't see them past the edge of the desk. As much as I hated him, I needed Harvey right now.

"It isn't just the hair color either, sweetheart. Saying your last films were B-rated is like saying root canal surgery is a pleasant way to spend an afternoon. Three of them were so bad they died untimely deaths in the cutting room, never even made it past editing before they were canned. Those included the two you had the lead role in. That's hardly a selling point in Hollywood, kiddo."

Ouch. I dropped back in the hard chair that sat across from his desk, and tried to decide whether to punch him in the face or ask for a loan to get a boob job and dye my hair. Maybe I should just take what he was offering me. But it somehow sounded shady. "I'm not doing porn, Harvey."

He guffawed. "With a name like Kitty French, you could."

The urge to slap him returned, but his chuckle faded and he waved the air as though to clear my concerns. "There's no sex. This is all high-class stuff, I swear!" Harvey swiped an X across his heart with a finger. Or at least where his heart would be if he had one. "Okay, okay, you're going to get guys nibbling on you a bit. That's a given, it's vampires for crissakes. But nothing more serious than that."

I should hold my ground. I should demand a real acting job, in a real production, but the words wouldn't come out. Only excuses flew through my mind. I wasn't good enough. I needed any money I could get.

"How much does it pay?"

"Two grand. Are you in?"

My eyes popped. That was more than I was expecting, especially for a late notice gig.

I said yes, what else could I say? The money

Harvey offered would be enough to cover rent and ensure I could eat something besides ramen noodles cooked by soaking them in cold water on a hot patio. If it were as tame and easy as Harvey promised, maybe I could even turn it into a regular gig. I could get my own place, cover my living costs while trying to get real acting work. Maybe it would all turn out fine.

A girl had to hold onto hope.

2

The venue for the LARP event, a club called *Dark Raine*, surprised me. It was all class, with shining black marble floors, and sparkling crystal chandeliers, cozy nooks for couples sharing cocktails, and businessmen unwinding after work. A young man in a tailored black uniform that matched the décor greeted me at the door. After my bewildered explanation of why I was there, he directed me to the third floor.

Stepping off the elevator, it felt as though I'd walked onto the set of a classic Hammer horror film, with billowing, tattered curtains, black leather furniture, and huge candelabras with candles guttering in their grips. They looked like diseased trees, and I felt a tingle of unease run down my back. A woman claiming to be the event liaison directed me to the dressing room and handed me my costume. The flowing, medieval style chemise was of a fabric that was just transparent enough to make you question what you were seeing through it, and torn strategically to show off legs all the way to the hip. An ivory corset went over that, and the woman helped lace me up, leaving the top few eyelets at the front undone so the spill of cleavage was accentuated.

It was too late for second thoughts, but I was having them anyway. Maybe it was the scantiness of the costume, or the fact that I was beginning to wonder if there really was a porn movie in the making here, despite what Harvey promised me.

Thankfully, the event liaison confirmed that participants weren't allowed to take off clothes—mine or theirs. Though they were allowed to touch and bite a little.

Two other girls were there waiting, looking bored, as though they'd done this a million times already. One gave me a nod and little wink, then chuckled at her own joke about me being new blood. I grinned politely in return. Seeing I wasn't the only victim for the event calmed me a little, until the paranoia that this was really a porn shoot came back. The winky woman was already in her costume and went to take up her starting spot in another room. Her ass was entirely visible through the sheer fabric of her gown. I looked again at the fabric of my chemise and hoped it wasn't the same.

Adding to my discomfort was my overfull belly, squeezed into the corset. That was entirely my own fault. Harvey had given me a rather tidy advance on the two thousand I would be making. I made for the nearest steakhouse so fast I'm surprised I didn't run down a few diners trying to get into the place. Oysters on the half shell for starters, then a perfectly rare filet mignon with roasted asparagus. I managed to refrain from dessert, thanks somewhat to common sense kicking in, reminding me not to blow my new windfall too fast. But mostly, it was on account of being entirely too full. Totally worth it though.

I was given my directions and starting position. *It's just like any other acting job*, I tried to comfort myself, *with a lot more improv.*

At least it would bring in some money and wasn't quite porn. I'm not sure if that would make my mom feel any prouder if she found out about this little escapade. *She will never know about it,* I promised myself.

I lay on a vintage chaise lounge, awaiting the vampire hordes. Above me, the red lights flickered, and a soundtrack of distant thunder played through hidden speakers nearby. A whisper of a shiver ran

up my spine. I was doing my best to get into my role while I waited for the players to appear, and the effects they had set up for the event did a decent job of building the mood. The décor was a little over the top and cliché, from the smoke machine mist drifting across the floor, to the lights flashing behind fake windows, to simulate lightening. The expense put into the event startled me, and that wasn't even counting my wage for the night, or that of the other victims.

The lights flickered again and I stared upward, my body going rigid as the first rustles sounded in the distance. They were coming. Despite being told what to expect, I was nervous. A deep animal instinct welled up in me, and it was all I could do not to run. But I'd committed to this crazy job, and I was going to be professional about it. I would run, but not until the players were ready to chase me. I swallowed hard and focused on the prize, the cute little one-bedroom place I had checked out that afternoon. It was in West Hollywood, not far from where I currently lived, but it would be just mine. Not sharing with nine other people would also make it easier to date again, or even just hook up more often. I hadn't been laid in forever. My living conditions weren't entirely at fault though. I worked too hard on getting my career off the ground, and seemed to have the worst taste in guys.

unLife

My last boyfriend had been a down and out loser by anyone's standards. Seth, with his leather jacket, motorcycle, and nasty habit of borrowing money. By the time I kicked him out of my life, he owed me over five thou. That wasn't the only reason our relationship had ended though. He was a poet, and had always insisted that he needed certain things to feel inspired. Alcohol and sex, primarily. Apparently, that's how he ended up in the woman's restroom at open mic night with a woman named Irene.

I should know by now that bad boys are just that—bad.

The air conditioning chilled the room, making goosebumps spread across my bulging cleavage and bare thigh. My cheeks flushed at the thought that I was about to be set upon by a stranger, lying here so exposed. Not that I hadn't done physical contact and sex scenes before, but the lack of cameras, crew, and director made it feel off. You'd think having an audience would make it feel weirder, but the lack of one was worse.

The rustling grew louder, and I threw an arm dramatically over my forehead and feigned sleep. From beneath the shadow of my arm, I cracked open my eyelids to watch what was going on. The dark deepened, and a tall figure came at me from the shadows. I shrieked, and it wasn't fake. Adrenaline spurted into my bloodstream. I hurled myself off the lounge, running for the double doors to the right. It was just a game, but between the suddenness of it all and the darkness that seemed more sinister than it had a moment ago, I felt real fear. My logical brain reminded me that the club had security watching in case someone went too far, but terror made me panic as the man chased me around the room. Curtains swirled about me like caressing ghosts, disorienting me as I spun around and came face-to-face with the vampire.

I almost laughed. Okay, yeah, I did laugh. So much for staying professional. A guy that looked like a friendly accountant peered at me. He had a little bit of a paunch that spilled over his burgundy cummerbund. Contact lenses made his eyes a rich red, and he wore gothic clothing with a long cape and stiff high collar. He bared his fangs, waggling his eyebrows at me from under a heavy coating of glitter. *Oh, THAT kind of vampire.* I wasn't so scared anymore.

He hissed and drew his ridiculously long cape over his face like a wannabe Bela Lugosi. I faked a swoon, letting my eyelashes flutter dramatically against my cheeks. My knees bent as though about to give way. He reached out to grab me, but I ran into the next room with a girly shriek. I swear I heard him chuckle as I fled. He followed slowly, enjoying the chase. I wouldn't admit it aloud, but I was almost starting to enjoy myself. Acting was my passion, and even something as nonsensical as this stirred my blood. I let myself get into it. I tapped into the hundreds of horror movies I'd watched, calling on that archetypal, innocent, Victorian maiden stereotype that seemed so omnipresent.

I dodged between tattered curtains, the smell of dust and rain swirling through the air. *Did someone open a window?* Maybe my imagination was running away with me. I could hear the sounds of the club downstairs over the fake thunder and noise of a downpour. I nearly crashed into a candelabra and paused to catch my breath, looking around wide-eyed and panting. A slight shift in a shadow caught my attention, and another dark figure appeared. This one had a bit more going for him in terms of being tall, dark, and deadly serious. He extended a hand toward me, each finger tipped with a long, sharp nail. I hoped they were fake. I watched his hand for a moment as though mesmerized.

Then I shook my head and bolted, going for the first set of doors I could see. I sure was getting my cardio today. My pulse roared in my ears, my heart pounding in my chest.

The next room was set up like a Victorian banquet hall, complete with a long dining table and roaring fireplace. As I ran in, two more men appeared out of the shadows, swooping at me. I was seized on both sides and lifted off my feet as I screamed. I

struggled, but the men kept a strong grip on me as they laid me on the dining table. I was supine, pinned down, at the mercy of three vampires. *It's okay. They aren't real. Just men playing a game.*

That didn't stop my gut reaction. I tugged my arm, and one of the vampires had a hard time holding me down. I relaxed slightly. Those hours at the gym have helped, but I was being paid to play a victim. Knowing I could probably break free if things got out of hand did make me feel better. I just had to be careful not to make them feel less powerful. They wanted to feel like they were in control. I continued to squirm and struggle weakly, still panting from my adrenaline driven sprint. My torn gown crept up as I kicked, leaving my legs bare.

A tongue licked across the lowest point of my neck, right where my pulse beat. A frisson of desire ran through my body, startling me. I reminded myself this was just a job. *Stay professional.*

The vampire-men crowded around the table, crawling onto it to get better access to me. I was dinner for them tonight. A hot mouth met my cleavage. I gasped at the sensation, then screamed. I wanted to strike the man off me but stayed in character. It wasn't the first time I'd put up with being kissed or fondled for a scene. Hell, my first big part had been a high school student making out with her boyfriend in a car. I died in the first five minutes of the movie. Standard old slasher pic. That had been one of the ones that had gotten all the way through production. And straight to DVD.

My mind wandered as I tried to relax into the role and let the men play their vampire game with my body.

Then one of them bit me.

He didn't bite hard, but he wasn't exactly gentle either. *That's going to leave a mark.* I was sprawled on the table, teeth nipping at me in three places. Their plaything. I let myself go limp with a quiet moan like a victim finally overcome. I silently congratulated myself on how realistic it sounded. Hot hands tangled into my hair, and warm tongues slid across my skin. Someone tugged my hair a little harder and I gasped, arching my back. I suddenly realized there was a reason for the highly sexual reaction to vampires as portrayed in so many movies. This was surprisingly, undeniably, *hot.* Fake fangs pulled at the bared flesh of my cleavage, arms and neck. Little shivers stole up and down my spine, making me whimper, and a delicious ache built inside me. It was so unexpectedly provocative I hardly realized I'd almost entirely lost my composure. I was legitimately beginning to enjoy myself, and not just because I loved acting. I had just about decided that I really needed to get laid soon, when an icy finger ran up my thigh, yanking me out of the delectable stupor I had tumbled into.

I felt a cold nose press against my neck and breathe deeply. I heard a small grunt of desire.

"Stop. This one is mine." The smooth, cultured voice seemed to spear through my body, deep and commanding.

My eyelids, gone heavy during the biting, flew open to see my vampires backing away. Their faces had gone blank. It looked like someone had reached in and erased them from within. Lights on, nobody home.

A new man stood above me at the side of the table, silhouetted by the dim scarlet glow of the lamp behind him.

Just another player? Something seemed different, and a primal instinct to escape invaded me again. I tried to scramble away across the table, but icy cold hands dragged me back and up into his arms. *I'm hallucinating*, I insisted to the panicking, animal instinct in my brain. He was probably wearing cooling gloves, or something to give the illusion of being corpselike. A hardcore player, more so than the other vampires who had fallen back. Except that even in the dim light, I knew he wasn't wearing gloves. His lips whispered against the side of my neck. I shivered at the coolness of his breath. He was stronger too. No matter how much I struggled against him, I couldn't get his fingers to budge. It was like he was made of stone.

I heard him inhale deeply, his mouth just below

my ear.

Then his teeth sunk deep into my neck.

This was no small bite. Pain went from searing hot to icy cold, both sides of it so intense I screamed in agony. I closed my eyes as the pain made my vision swim, threatening my consciousness with the sudden fierce agony. I thrashed and kicked, but his arms locked my upper body in place. I flailed my hands ineffectually, trying to push him off. I could feel the blood leaving my body in the strangest sort of internal suction. Gradually, my struggle lessened, no strength left. My throat grew hoarse from screaming. Dizziness overwhelmed me.

The silent players stood there, watching vacantly. I stared at their emptied out faces over the attacker's shoulder, wondering where the help I had been promised was, how this could be happening. Was I going to die?

My fingers curled weakly in the fabric of my attacker's shirt, still feebly trying to pull him off me, or maybe just trying to steady myself as the world spun away. It was getting hard to think, like my brain was filling with fog and cobwebs.

Fake lightning. Fake mist. Real blood.

Darkness rushed up from the floor.

I saw one last candle, spitting its fire in the grotesque candelabra, then everything went black.

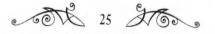

3

eath ... death is ... Death tastes like coconut.
Wetness, on my lips, on my chin.

I opened my eyes as coconut water dribbled from my slackly open mouth. It was being fed to me by a blank-eyed creature with a nest of black hair, the grey face of an English schoolmarm, and a wide, wicked grin. Her lips were coated in blood red lipstick, so badly applied it smeared up her cheeks and on her teeth. At least, I hoped it was lipstick.

What is going on? Am I dreaming?

The last thing I remembered ... I had been bitten. Bitten by what, a real vampire? All reality and reason had fled my world. Vampires didn't exist. I, Kitty French, did not believe in hocus pocus like that. I was a thoroughly modern woman. I was simply in the grasp of some lunatic who believed himself to be a blood drinker.

Thirst raged in me. I didn't know what was happening, but if I was thirsty, I couldn't be dead. I tried to focus on the room I was in, but pain sank like talons into my throat, wrists, and shoulders.

"Hrrrgggh," I got out before the woman doused me again, the juice spilling from the spoon and onto my chin. My tongue instinctively shot out, lapping at the liquid trickling down my face. It wasn't enough to soothe my parched throat. My vision was fuzzy but gradually starting to clear. If I didn't struggle and didn't move my head much, the pain faded to a throb that I could handle. Barely.

I hung from my wrists against a wall. My arms restrained above my head. I stared upwards at the complicated contraption of heavy black chains connected to a pulley system. Looking up made my neck ache and stab with pain, so I let my chin drop and stared ahead, trying to see what else I could find out. My toes curled against cold tiles, and I realized I was able to touch the floor and that my ankles weren't shackled. I had been hanging limply, all my weight on my wrists, but now I was coming back to my senses I set the balls of my feet on the ground. My legs wobbled weakly but took my weight. I almost cried in relief as the strain lessened.

I looked wildly around, trying to work out where

unlife

I was. I was surrounded by kitchen appliances I would have envied if I had not been scared shitless. The granite countertops were immaculate, and the chefs' knives displayed along a magnetic strip on the wall looked expensive. The irony was that I was in, without a doubt, my dream kitchen. Except that I was strung up from the wall instead of the fine hunk of cured Spanish pork that should have been there.

The woman who looked like Halloween warmed over, spoon feeding me coconut juice, was also out of place. She belonged in a haunted library, or a rundown, creepy sideshow. Not what appeared to be a fairly modern high-end home. The rich colors in the cherry cabinets, and slate tiled floor, seemed to wash her out further. Her blank look jarred my memory. The fake vampires had worn that same look when the one with the cold hands, and really sharp teeth, had appeared …

Movement. My gaze whipped to the left and there he was.

I'd half expected to see a grotesque monster. The media had shown so many types of vampires over the years, that when presented with what could potentially be the real thing, I didn't know what to expect. *Not that there is such a thing as the real thing,* I tried to tell myself, not sure what my foggy brain believed at this point, but it seemed sensible to try and hold onto logic a little longer. Regardless of whether he was monster or man, he was surprising.

Only the white, lifeless skin made him seem anything but human. It was pristine, like alabaster or fresh, unyellowed ivory. The kind of skin Victorian women and goths would have killed for. He had deep brown, swept back hair. The color was too rich to be mistaken for black. It was like really good, really dark chocolate. His eyes were fringed with lashes so thick it looked like he was wearing mascara and so long that when he blinked, they seemed to brush his cheeks. His face was built of sharp angles and high cheekbones.

His long body was clothed in all black: silk shirt clinging to his broad shoulders and accentuating his narrow waist, and black jeans that outlined his lean legs and hips. He couldn't be anything but human. When I met his eyes though, there was nothing there. No humanity, not even curiosity. No soul.

This man's eyes were a true void-like black. Deep and endless, they drew me in, inhuman and so cold I felt goose bumps shiver up my skin.

Under normal circumstances I would have found him desperately handsome. But not now. Not this inhuman thing that all parts of my being wanted to run from. When I looked at him, my body screamed *PREDATOR*, sending off alerts through all my internal systems.

He stared hungrily at me, like a chef preparing

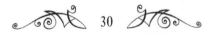

a particularly expensive cut of meat. At least it appeared to me that the sensual way he ran his eyes over my body was akin to the way I eyed rich ice cream.

"You need to stay hydrated. The coconut water will help. Drink," he said.

The spoon actually made it between my lips. I swallowed greedily. I needed to get rid of the burning in my throat. One spoonful wasn't enough, but it did help.

He nodded. "Good girl." His condescending voice prickled the hairs on the back of my neck and made my face twist into a snarl.

Not doing it for you, monster.

I glared at him, hating that he ordered me to do the thing I wanted and needed. Hating that I couldn't refuse him. Anger rose in me. I despised this creature thoroughly, and I was already planning what would happen when I escaped. I was going to report his kidnapping ass to the police and enjoy it when they dragged him off to rot in jail.

The kitchen was lit by weak, early morning sunlight, but he stood in a small pool of shadows, his face turned away from the windows. The cedar shades allowed dusty bars of lemony yellow light in. I stared at it, trying to think past the immediate situation and to my future survival.

I managed to look down at the condition of my

body. My corset was stained where dried blood pooled on one of my breasts. I didn't feel pain or signs of violation anywhere except my neck, and was glad that all my clothing was still on. That was a start. The amount of dried blood worried me though, and the dizziness I was fighting made a little more sense. How much blood had I lost?

More juice hit my cheek. "Sstaaa...." My throat was so sore I couldn't speak. My hand automatically tried to go there, to comfort the wound. The chains made a musical rattle of protest at the motion, and the reality of my situation struck me hard.

I'm someone's prisoner. Some monster's prisoner.

Terror exploded inside me. Black, blinding terror that sent me into a writhing, kicking, scratching, frenzy that was short-lived due to the fact that I could not scream nor move in any real direction, and the only thing the thrashing accomplished was to make my arms and shoulders ache even more. My wrists felt the strain as I scrambled to find my footing again and ease the pain. Exhaustion and despair poured through me in waves.

Tears seeped from my eyes, but I blinked them back. I wouldn't let that monster see me weak. I managed to scrape out a raspy, "Why?"

It was a damn good question. I mean, all I had done was try to earn a living. No way did I deserve to be chained up in a vampire's kitchen.

unLife

No, just a vampire poser, I reminded my blurring brain. I was thinking of him as a real monster because I hated the idea a human would do this to me. But I knew the world was full of human monsters who would do this and worse. My eyes went back to his ghastly pallor and the way he stood so far back in the shadows. Maybe he was just a whack job who had taken the whole thing too seriously. Looking at the woman who was haphazardly feeding me, I thought she could be a junkie. Then again, the players at the LARP scene had definitely not been junkies. There hadn't been time to slip them something. Hypnotism maybe?

If I could accept hypnotism as an excuse, I might as well believe it was real vampiric compulsion, just like I've seen in so many movies. Could he be a real vampire and the woman his human thrall? My mind was going back and forth like a ping-pong ball.

I didn't know. I couldn't know. I wanted some other explanation, so I asked again, "Why?"

"What's your favorite food?"

I stared at him, bewildered by the response. And what a question to ask a die-hard foodie. What was my favorite food? Lobster tail drowning in fresh drawn butter, couscous plump and rich with leeks and the mildest of cheeses? Maybe simple freshly baked bread still warm from the oven, its outside brown and crisp and its middle delightfully chewy,

slathered in the best French butter? The strangeness of the question sent my mind into a tailspin.

He didn't seem to take my not answering as an offense. "Mine is strawberries. Or, it was, back when I could still partake in food."

I was confused. Why would I care what his favorite food was? I could understand why he was asking about mine. Perhaps this was like death row, and I was going to get a first-class meal before he punched my exit ticket to the next world, but why was he telling me about his? If he really was a vampire, then I already knew what his current favorite food was.

He tilted his head, examining me with dark eyes. "If you found a strawberry plant that grew the most exquisite berries in the world, so ripe, so plump, so perfectly sweet with just a hint of tartness lurking in their firm red flesh, would you strip it bare? Would you tear it up from the roots to gorge yourself on the fruit? No, you would tend it, care for it, so it would stay alive, and continue to grow and bear fruit so you could savor the taste of its berries until the end of its short season."

I didn't like where this was going. My head shook side to side, denying him. I refused to draw the parallels he was trying to make.

His eyes met mine, their black so deep, gaze so empty of soul or emotion that my whole body shuddered in fear and revulsion. "You are my strawberry. I will keep you alive as long as possible, and you will be my only food until you finally die. There is something about your blood, something so delicious I can't bear to part with you or consume you all in one meal. I aim to have you as long as possible."

I couldn't speak. I could do nothing but stare at him. Was this really going to be my fate? Run away from my family to a place I had no friends, to work for a few years in meaningless roles, and then die to some crazy? Some monster who thought I *tasted* good?

I didn't have to respond, because he turned away, then said over his shoulder, "It is too late in the morning for me to have any strength left. I will see you this evening." Then he disappeared, as though he had never been there at all.

See me for what? Dinner? My neck ached, and the thrall dipped the spoon into the juice again, splattering it against the side of my nose. With the vampire gone, she stood there confused for a moment then walked away, her arms and legs jerking like a possessed marionette that had been let off its strings. I stared at the remains of the coconut water, lying just out of reach. It was all I could do not to whine like an abandoned dog.

I watched as the woman started to clean the kitchen, and it became clear she wasn't going to come back to feed me. I called to her, begged her for help, for freedom, for my life, scratching my tender

throat bare. She made no sign she even knew I was there as she mechanically scrubbed the counters. Then she left the room with a vacuum cleaner tucked under her arm, carrying it like a load of groceries.

Alone in the kitchen, I let myself cry. Tears trickled down my cheeks, stinging the wound on my throat as the moisture loosened the dried, caked blood. I could only imagine how I looked, mascara running down my face, one side of my body drizzled in blood. I forced myself to settle, blinking rapidly and sniffing hard to stop my nose from running. Hanging around indulging in a big tear-fest was only wasting time. Tears wouldn't help me now. What would help was to get out of these chains and out of this crazy house. My eyes went to the rack of kitchen knives on the wall nearby. I glanced up at the pulley system, trying to judge how far it would let me move. If I could reach a thin fillet knife, I could try to open the cuffs that were against my wrists. And if that didn't work, maybe I could defend myself against the vampire when he came back to eat me.

The chains had some give, and when I pulled hard, they ran through the pulley system and let me bring my arms down, but it took a lot of effort. When I didn't pull hard enough, the pulley started reeling me back in. My muscles shook and strained from the effort. The metal made a harsh whispering sound as I tried to creep along the floor to the counter. I was brought up abruptly by the bonds though, just inches from the counter and the knives. I strained against the shackles with everything I had, bracing against the wall with my feet, hoping they would break or come undone, but that only exhausted me. The chains reeled me back in and left me hanging with my face pressed into the cold tiles of the wall.

There was blood there. Dried and flaked, much older than anything I might have left behind. *I'm not the first victim.* Is this where the other girls ended up? The ones Harvey had sent out that never came back?

My head buzzed and there was a distant roaring in my ears. Something warm and thick dripped down the side of my neck, soaking the top of my chemise and corset. I'd torn my abused neck open again and it bled freely. The light faded out around the edges of my sight and I groaned, too weak to keep on fighting although every part of me wanted to. The last thing I saw was the thrall, with her clown-from-planet-crazy smile, coming closer. Strange, I hadn't even heard her come back. Had she been watching me this whole time?

Don't bite me, you bitch.

Then I was gone.

4

There was a sound, a slow, soft sound that made me raise my head. Darkness surrounded me, and I hung limp from my bonds. All my senses were numbed, but I could tell I was dehydrated, starving, and nearly bled out. I fought death with every fragment of strength left in me but felt it creeping into my core. More than anything I felt cold. My muscles ached with the intensity of the shivers that rattled my body. The movement beat the chains against each other in a discordant cacophony.

My eyelids drooped and I dragged them back up, seeing only short blinks of the last moments of my life.

The thrall stood beside me, wiping a spot on the counter over and over, her face caught in that same wicked expression. As I drifted in and out of consciousness, I swear I caught her shooting looks at me, sly little glances. The kitchen was eerily dark, and not just around the edges of my vision. It was lit by slivers of silver moonlight trickling through the blinds, sapping the color out of the world.

A light came on. The vampire appeared.

He looked at the scene before him, and his expression changed to something fierce and dangerous. His entire body seemed to thrum like a taut bowstring. I could almost feel the carefully restrained violence. Except that I couldn't really *feel* anything. Even that realization seemed distant and dreamlike.

He shouted at the thrall. His words, and all other sounds around me, were muffled, and I couldn't make them out. But the vampire's words seemed to affect her like a wave of force. She turned and ran, frantically and madly, colliding face first with the wall.

She twisted and crumpled. Blood broke from her nose but she never made a sound. I shuddered helplessly. She rolled over to the counter then got to her feet, still smiling her ghastly ghoulish grin, a trickle of blood running down the side of her mouth. She skulked away, looking back over her shoulder until he roared at her again and she left at a ragged trot.

UnLife

He was beside me faster than I knew how. His fingers pressed against my pulse and he cursed. I tried to speak, to ask for mercy but there was nothing left in me. My breath simply wheezed out, wordless. He broke the cuffs with one movement and I fell into his arms. *How could he be so fast, so strong? How could I ever hope to escape if he was strong enough to break steel?*

That was when I knew for sure. I knew, no matter what this man was, he was not human.

He lifted me in a swift, gentle movement. I rolled weakly into his chest, feeling the strength of his muscles as he carried me through the huge house. His body was cold, so cold it sent shivers down my spine.

The world blurred around me, then I found myself being carefully laid down on a bed. I sank into a soft mattress covered with silky sheets. A cool night breeze came from somewhere, and my teeth chattered violently.

The vampire left me like that, vanishing again. I wasn't restrained. I tried to move my feet, my hands, but could not muster the energy. I lay there weak and senseless. *This is my only chance at escape and I'm blowing it!* The anger that surged into me at that thought gave me a second wind and I rolled onto my side.

Before I could even attempt to put a foot on the floor, he was back.

41

He held a tray filled with gauze padding, bandages, and a handcuff. I wanted to fight him, but it was all I could do to stay conscious. My fingers fluttered in weak protests against his hands, trying to fend off the new cuff. My wrists were chafed from my struggles and hanging in the unforgiving manacles. Welts had formed where they had been abraded the worst. He caught my hands in an iron grip. He placed the thin cuff of gleaming steel around one of my wrists and ran a very long, thin chain through it. He locked it to the bed neatly. I stared up at the shifting shadows on the ceiling and began to weep softly, unable to hold it in any longer. I was completely at the mercy of this monster. I was just so tired. I wanted to be home in my bed with a pillow crammed over my head, wishing my rock-star wannabe roommates would shut up so the rest of us could get some sleep.

But I wasn't at home. The world swam around me, even my mind was lost for a moment in the agony.

The vampire dipped his head toward me. *This is it*, I thought wildly, my foggy brain not even pausing to wonder why he would chain up someone he intended to kill now. Any doubts I'd had about his status as inhuman fled my mind under the cold touch of his fingers. The touch of his tongue against my neck startled me, but I couldn't do anything but twitch and shake. With long, sure strokes, he lapped the blood from my throat and collarbone. His soft murmur of pleasure left me feeling sick.

After he pulled his face away, lips red with my blood, his long and elegant fingers stroked my neck, pressing some stinking ointment into the wound. Pain sizzled along my nerve endings. I passed out momentarily but came back to find him bandaging my neck with the same gentleness he had used to carry me to the room.

But there was no gentleness in his eyes. They were still empty, calculating. It was the gaze of a predator making sure its food supply remained viable. He'd told me he would tend to me like a strawberry plant, and here he was, trying to repot me after I'd been ripped out of the ground.

More coconut water appeared, and the vampire spooned it slowly through my cracked lips. Unlike the thrall, not a drop spilled on me, and I sipped it slowly, letting it replenish me. I needed my strength because I intended to do everything I could to stay alive. I didn't know how much time I would have, but I wanted every minute of it. The longer I could stay alive, the longer I had to figure out how to escape. I still felt so weak though, wavering in and out of consciousness.

He sat beside me, feeding me silently for what felt like hours. I may have slept at some point, but couldn't tell, because whenever I was awake, he was there, tenderly caring for my wound or rehydrating me spoon by spoon.

A small glow of light warmed the room. It came from wide double doors, open and leading to a balcony from the huge bedroom. I had some strength back, and when the vampire tried to feed me again, I pushed him away, took the cup from the table, and drank it myself.

He brushed tangled hair away from my face. His hand was soft but cold, and he murmured words that were hardly reassuring. "I thought I'd lost you, my Strawberry. I was careless for not giving my maid stricter instructions on how to look after you. But you are revived, and I will see you stay healthy. I intend to feed from your delicious blood many more times before you die."

How thoughtful, I wanted to snark at him, but fear held my tongue. *There have been times I've had some deep and intimate feelings for chocolate, but I still ate it all up till it was gone.*

"How can you treat me like this?" My throat throbbed, and I wasn't sure if it was from all the screaming or the bite in the side of it.

His gaze held mine, empty and cold. "You're nothing but food to me."

I searched for something in his expression that said otherwise, but only saw the monster, only that inhuman, unfeeling stare. But he seemed at least logical, ethical even, in the treatment of his 'food'. Maybe I could convince him to see me as something more than a meal. If he could see me as a living, feeling person, surely he would let me go free.

I grasped at that, desperate words spilling from my lips. "My name is Kitty. Kitty French. I'm an actress, I live in West Hollywood. And since you asked, my idea of a damn fine meal is rare steak with shavings of black truffle and triple cooked potato." My throat ached with each word, but I couldn't seem to stop them. And I knew I shouldn't speak, I should save my strength, but I had to try to make myself seem more human and less vampire cuisine.

A strange fury filled the vampire's eyes, and he stood up from the side of the bed. He stormed to the door. My plan to appeal to him had failed. At least him leaving might give me the chance to escape.

At the doorway he hesitated. He spoke over his shoulder. "Owen Raine. That's my name, Strawberry."

"That's not *my* name, Vampire."

The corner of his lips twitched. *A smile?* He glanced at the balcony and the brightening sky beyond, then left without another word. I latched on to that fleeting smirk, hoping I hadn't imagined it. If he had a sense of humor, maybe he wasn't completely out of reach. The ability to laugh, to feel at all, was something so human that it had to mean he wasn't completely monstrous.

"Owen." I rolled the name off my tongue like a promise. That I would not call him by his name until he called me by mine. I was not his strawberry. I would make him know me, see me. It might be the only chance I had to survive.

5

I watched the open door he'd gone through while the sunrise brought thin beams of warmth into the room. The smell chlorine and the sea floated in on the breeze. *He has a pool and we're near the ocean?* He had to be loaded. Or maybe, the house belonged to the thrall or some other victim of his. It was hard to say. The world had gone crazy, or I had. Vampires were real and I was at the mercy of one. I thought through all the tales of crosses, stakes to the heart, garlic, transforming into bats, and sleeping in coffins, creating a mental file of stuff pop culture had told me about vampires. There must be some weakness I could exploit that applied to the real thing. Daylight hurting them seemed true enough. Owen obviously avoided it, but he seemed able to deal with indirect sunlight, hiding in the shadows. Other than that, I had little idea what kind of creature I was *really* dealing with. But logic said he was going to be sleeping all day, which meant I might actually be able to get away from him. This was my chance, not to be wasted as the earlier one had been.

My wrist was still caught in the silver loop of the cuff, and when I sat up a slight dizziness washed over me. I was still weak, but who knows how weak I would be tomorrow, or the next day, slowly being drunk dry. I did feel stronger than a few hours ago. I tried not to dwell on the way I shook every time I moved, and the way the world swam when I sat up.

My first move was to find the bathroom. The need to escape getting trumped momentarily by the need to pee.

Swinging my legs off the side of the bed and trying to stand showed me just how weak I was. I prided myself on my working out. After all, I loved a good dessert, and if I was going to make it big as an actress, I had to work off that slice—or three—of cheesecake after dinner. *Oh, cheesecake.* Thinking about it made my stomach rumble. Now that my thirst was mostly quenched, I suddenly became aware of how horribly hungry I was. If the night before last had been the night after the LARP, then it was going on thirty-six hours since my decadent meal. It seemed far longer than that though, as though the steakhouse existed in a different lifetime. I was starving. Anything to eat would have been good, even if it was just a packet of instant ramen.

My legs were shaky and I had to sit back down, take a few breaths, then stand again. Three false starts later I staggered across the room, the chain dragging behind me. It was clearly long enough to let me move freely within the confines of my cell, but I doubted I'd make it much farther. The chain was thin but the sheer length of it made it heavy. I barely felt like I had the strength to lift my arm. The loop of metal that closed around my wrist was smooth and polished, pressing into my skin with surprisingly little discomfort.

"I feel like a damn dog," I muttered as I stepped into the bathroom. Out of some sense of privacy I tried to close the door, but it wouldn't quite shut with the chain in the way. I left it ajar, too tired to bother with it.

I immediately forgot my anger at the sight of the exquisite marble tiling, floor to ceiling mirrors, thick Turkish towels, and a huge tub that looked like it could hold a party of four. I bet the tub was real marble too. The stone was cold under my feet and made me shake, remembering the deadly cold that had crept through my body earlier. I wanted to soak in that tub, immersed in hot water to chase the chill away.

The toilet was hidden behind a tiny partition and I stumbled to it, pulled down my panties, plopped onto the seat and sighed with relief, until I looked up and caught my reflection in the mirror.

My face was streaked with dried tears. My hair was a rat's nest, the blue-black waves sticking up in dry hunks and tangles around my paler than usual face. My lips were normally rosy, but they were a bleached-out gash. My eyes had dark shadows below them, and my neck had a huge purple-yellow bruise around the carefully wrapped bandage. Dried blood crusted the front of my costume, and sweat stains showed under my arms. The mascara that had been thickly applied for the game had migrated below my eyes, enhancing how sunken they were. All my other makeup seemed to have smeared off at some point during my ordeal.

I looked like hell.

And I stank.

The smell hit me all at once and I gagged. I stared at the tub, a deep longing for a good soak sinking into me. I could imagine how it would feel in there, up to my neck in hot water made fragrant and silky by the jars of bath oils that lined the tub's edge. This time though, the longing wasn't for the warmth but for cleanliness. I fantasized for a moment how it would feel to scrub myself off in the gently perfumed water and then step out, snuggling into one of those plush white towels. Every part of me longed for comfort.

But there was no time to clean up now. I had to push my thoughts forward, toward escape. Until then, maybe my offensive odor would make me less of a tasty treat.

I set my jaw hard in resolve, imagining a future where I survived, where I would have the comfort I yearned for. *When I'm free again. When I'm free I'll have the most perfect bath ever.* I ignored the fact that the tiny bathroom I shared with a bunch of other people wasn't anything like this. It didn't even have a tub. It had a grimy shower stall full of other peoples' stuff.

Cleaning up wasn't in the plan, but I considered that getting more clothing would be useful. The long, flowy chemise and corset were not practical for escape attempts at all. A pair of pants would have been just my cup of tea right then, or at least a shirt. Anything to get the blood crusted thing off me and make me feel a little less exposed.

I limped back out to the bedroom. In the daylight the furnishings made me stare. The bed was a huge four poster, the carpet plush and soft. My toes sank into the pile, welcome warmth after the coolness of the bathroom tile. A leather sofa sat in one corner below deep windows, and one wall was lined with bookshelves. From the placement of the window in the bathroom and on two walls in here, I had to be in a corner room of the building.

Testing the boundaries of my leash, I found I could reach all parts of the bathroom, and bedroom but not the balcony. I could make it through the bedroom door to the top of a large staircase made of teak and surrounded by a black wrought iron railing. A hallway below seemed to go on forever, and I could see an immense modern living area down the stairs. It looked like something out of a magazine or hotel, dark leather couches with glass and black metal tables. The floor was hardwood to match the staircase with what looked like a real Persian rug laid under the coffee table. I couldn't quite reach the railing to look over it, but I could see broad double doors of solid wood—the entrance, or rather, exit? There were also several windows, giving me a glimpse of a driveway and a well-groomed front yard. I couldn't work out where the kitchen was. Reluctantly, I pulled my eyes away from the sunlight filtering in the front windows.

I searched for a tool or weapon I could use. The dresser drawers yielded nothing but a stray puff of dust and blank spaces. The armoire was also empty, so I was stuck in the vintage costume. Even the heavy side table was bare, not even a lamp. The room had the feel of one that was rarely, if ever, used, like a forgotten guest room. Only the bookshelf held anything at all, a dozen or so volumes. I tried wrenching the dresser apart, hitting it with a heavy book to smash free a sliver of wood to use as a stake, but I only succeeded in destroying the book. Looking down at the tattered pages, I sighed. It really was a shame, it looked like a fine old book. I tried not to feel bad about it. I wouldn't be destroying things if I hadn't been taken prisoner.

The chain was locked around a post of the bed with a huge and heavy padlock, and no matter what I tried it would not come loose of its mooring. In desperation, I planted my feet in a straddle-legged pose and tried to yank it free. *Fucking rich people, they never buy the flimsy pressed wood stuff.* While normally I would have approved, it certainly made my attempts to escape harder.

After a few minutes of straining, I gave up. The bed was solid and it wouldn't budge.

Or would it? If I could move it enough to get to the balcony, I could scream and wave for help. Surely a woman in a blood-soaked gown would attract some kind of attention. Even if I was at the back of the house, they might hear me. I was on the second story, so my voice should carry.

The bed was heavy as hell. I had to get behind it and push it inch by inch across the floor. It felt like it weighed more than a car. Frequently I had to stop and rest, leaning against it. I was grateful that the pitcher of coconut water had been left on the dresser

so I could continue to drink, otherwise I wouldn't have made any progress at all. The going was slow, but desperation is a great motivator. A few times, there were tearing sounds, and I grinned. *Screw that monster and his expensive carpet.*

The clock on the wall showed noon before I got the bed a few feet across the room, far enough that I could reach the French doors. I was shaking and covered in a fine sheen of sweat. Dots danced before my eyes, and my throat was sore again. I checked it gingerly. No blood was spurting out, that had to be a plus.

The balcony beckoned. I pushed the doors then stumbled out, only to stare in disbelief. I leaned on the railing, teeth gritted in frustration. The high hilltop was barren and isolated. The dun-colored slopes were covered in scrubby little bushes and stunted trees. The hills stretched away on either side without a single other building in sight. A thin gray ribbon of what had to be a private drive stretched for about a mile to a small highway below. The view was stark and beautiful. And we were completely alone.

I scanned the immediate area. A pool directly below was made to look like a river complete with waterfall, and not far past the property's boundary walls, a cliff dropped away to the sea. Around the other side was a tennis court, though the leaves gathered in the corners made me think it hadn't been used in years. I hadn't been quite right when

unLife

I thought I was in a corner room. The house was nestled into the hill, the levels distributed over the varying ground. The part of the house I was in was practically a tower that rose high above the surrounding, uninhabited landscape.

I screamed anyway, bellowing my cries for help into the wind. They blew back, uselessly. The caws of gulls in the distance seemed to mock me.

When I turned back to the bedroom, a tray of food sat on the bedside table. A shiver chilled me, wondering when it arrived, whether Owen could move about during the day, or if the creepy thrall had slunk in while I cried at the empty sky.

The serving tray held a still warm teapot that gave off the delicious odor of jasmine and vanilla, a plate on which rested a single slice of toast, neatly cut in triangular quarters, a tiny dish of jam, and a peeled and sectioned orange. The teapot, cup, plate, and dish were all made of safe, smooth edged metal. No cutlery, no ceramic or glass I could smash and use as a weapon, like I was some patient on suicide watch. If my captor was already thinking it, I wondered gloomily how long it would take me before I tried to kill myself as a form of escape. Not for a while. I wanted to live. And to live, I needed strength, and food.

I poured a cup of tea and tipped it back. I'd gone through all the coconut water and I was desperate

for a drink. It was heavenly on my tongue and soothed my throat. I would have liked some sugar, but there was none, so I dipped a finger into the jam and tasted it.

My eyes closed involuntarily in delight. Choke-cherries are almost inedible by themselves but they make an incredibly velvety jam. I dipped the toast into the jam pot, and gobbled down the orange, wiping my sticky fingers and mouth on the soft bedsheets as a small act of rebellion. I relished every bite. The bread was artisan, clearly fresh despite being toasted. It had been buttered lightly, and the faint hint of salt enhanced the sweetness of the grain and the jam that I dipped it in. The orange was succulent and perfectly ripe. Rarely did I get to eat this well. It was a welcome change from a diet heavy on beans, rice, and pasta.

Renewed, I considered my situation. I couldn't break the chain. I could find no weapon to defend myself with. I knew I was valued as food, but food doesn't get freedom. I needed to be seen as a human who deserved to be free. This morning I had received the vampire's name for my efforts. Maybe, if I kept playing on his sympathy, what little he had, I could achieve more. I was meant to be an actress after all.

This might be the role of a lifetime. Rather, it might be the role that saved my life.

6

The sun eventually dropped behind a bank of clouds. I watched it set, tears standing in my eyes at the beauty of it. Carnelian, pink, gold, and indigo blue lit the dome of the sky. Clouds, white and puffy, turned a brilliant orange and then a deep shade of lavender. *Would this be my final sunset?*

It reminded me in a lot of ways of the last sunset I'd seen back home. I'd watched it from the roof of my family's house. In the rural area where I had grown up, the sunsets were beautiful and pure. In the city, the sunset was spectacular for different reasons—pollution fogging the clouds and creating wild colors in the sky. It was a different kind of beauty; one I didn't appreciate nearly as much as the ones I'd grown up with. The breeze grew cold but I was reluctant to leave the fresh air that was as close to freedom as I could get.

The last ray of sunlight faded, and Owen appeared on cue. He eyed the room, the scraped carpet, the bed out of place. I stood defiant before him. The hell was I going to the effort of pushing that monster bed back to hide my escape efforts.

He tossed me onto the bed, and with one quick flick of his wrist the bed shot backwards, flying across the floor like an out-of-control rocket ship until it crashed against the wall. A startled scream escaped me, and I huddled next to the headboard, a white knuckled grip on one of the posts.

Before I knew it, the vampire was on top of me. He gripped my jaw in one hand, pressing my head back to inspect my neck. He tsked softly. "Strawberry, escape is not possible for you. I am not going to let you go, do you understand? All you will gain by attempting to escape is to cause yourself unnecessary pain."

The chill coming off his body was palpable. I put my best, most vulnerable, expression on, opening my mouth to begin a plea for my life, but it went still and silent on my tongue. He was looking directly at me, and his dark eyes were decidedly not human eyes, no mercy, no compassion lay in them. Nothing of that moment of hesitation and indecision I'd seen that morning. Nothing but a monster.

I squashed the shiver of fear in my gut. I was an

actor. I could transmute emotions the way alchemists were supposed to transmute lead into gold. I dug deep to find the rebellious teenager in me, channeling all my fear and desperation into bravado and anger.

I could strangle Owen with the chain, but I wasn't sure if he even needed to breathe. I stared daggers at him instead. "I will *never* stop trying to escape from you, monster."

His pale face didn't change expression, and I shuddered.

Owen moved off me casually, leaving in a blur and returning with a silver domed tray which he placed on the bedside table without ceremony. The mouthwatering aromas coming from the tray made my belly growl angrily. I didn't want the vampire to see me slobbering like one of Pavlov's dogs, so I focused my eyes elsewhere. That didn't do one ounce of good. I could smell truffle, butter and rare meat, and my stomach let out another loud and feral yelp.

Owen removed the dome to reveal the exact meal I had described myself as enjoying. An incredible slab of steak with an amount of fresh truffle shaved over the top that would cost me a few month's rent. The roast potatoes on the side looked fluffy and crunchy and golden through. For some reason, the meal choice infuriated me. I turned my back on it, and him, like a spoiled child. It also made me think. *He'd remembered.* Did that mean I was getting through to him? Or maybe he thought it was the most likely way to get me to eat something. Not that it would have taken much at this point with my stomach howling to be filled. Make no mistake, I was starving, and yet here I was being contrary. I never could be sensible.

"You must eat."

"So *you* can eat me?" I scoffed bitterly.

"Yes." His voice was crisp, with no hesitation as he answered me.

He was honest, I had to give him that.

"I'm not your food or your slave, Vampire. Think you can just put a nice meal in front of me and I'll be you're willing victim? Go fuck yourself." I knew I was goading him. It was a side of myself I was rarely brave enough to show, my sarcasm and snark normally hidden under fear of confrontation. But this monster had *imprisoned* me, and I had no desire to be polite to him.

Part of me almost hoped he would snap and kill me. I didn't want to die, but I wanted even less to be held prisoner so he could feed off me at his leisure. Another part of me was hoping to tease a reaction out of him. Any reaction that would show me there was still a man beneath the frigid, casually cruel exterior.

My words had no effect. He merely began to carve the hunk of Kobe beef into bite-sized bits. Juices ran across the plate, pooling nicely against the baked potato. The meat practically fell apart at the touch of the knife. I was certain it would melt like butter on my tongue.

"You must replenish your iron."

He tapped the fork against my lips. My traitorous mouth opened to accept the steak. My lips closed around it, and my eyelids fluttered as I savored the delicately seasoned morsel. I was such a sucker for good food. *If Owen doesn't kill me, I will likely die from over consumption.* It tasted as good as I imagined. Truffle was something I got so rarely that the taste always surprised me in the most delightful way. Earthy and rich, it mingled with the juicy steak.

The taste of the food made me realize how little I wanted to die. My life was precious. The thought startled me as I swallowed the first bite. I'd had so much to complain about lately. Failing career, absent relationships, infuriating housemates. I had worked my ass off to get where I wanted to be in life and hadn't gotten there. I felt like I wasn't getting anywhere. Faced with the possibility of dying, all of that seemed irrelevant. Sure, there were issues, my life was still a work in progress, but I loved being alive, experiencing every tiny, beautiful moment.

I opened my eyes and stared at Owen, my eyes tracing the curve of his cheek, the soft fan of his eyelashes as he looked down at the plate. How could a monster be so beautiful?

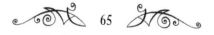

I rebelled with words only. "I'm not eating for you. Despite you being the devil for tempting me with this fucking incredible meal. I'm eating *for me*." I didn't have anything left to fight with but words at this point. I couldn't turn down the food. It was too good, and I was too hungry. At least with him feeding me, I could savor each bite. If I had control of the cutlery, I'd be stuffing my face in the least glamorous way. Owen's slow delivery of each bite was an exquisite kind of agony that nearly made me weep.

Still, I couldn't get any reaction from him. He was like an animated corpse, only caring about keeping his food supply viable. He placed another bite of the meat in my mouth, and I decided to try a different tactic. Time to switch acting roles.

I clutched at my stomach and buckled over onto the mattress in fake pain, crying out and writhing. Far from my best performance, it was still good enough to make Owen put down the steak knife to come to my aid.

"Strawberry, what's wrong?" His voice held no worry, more a clinical curiosity one might show a houseplant that wasn't growing well. He just didn't want his strawberry plant to stop fruiting so soon.

I rolled to the side. The knife was within reach. It was large and looked wickedly sharp.

While I still had the element of surprise, I grabbed it and stabbed it straight into his chest.

unLife

I worried that his body would somehow deflect the blade, like he was made of stone, but it didn't. The blade went in. At least, it went in a little way. His skin was cold, dense, and the blade lodged hard into it, blocked by muscle or ribcage below.

The knife may have stopped but my hand didn't. It kept going and my palm streaked along the razor-sharp edge. Blood swelled from the wound, dripping down his shirt front.

For a moment I just stared stupidly at my hand wrapped around the knife blade and the blood flooding out. More blood I didn't want to lose. Then the pain hit me.

I pulled my hand back, screaming, unable to bear the sight of my body losing more of the precious liquid that kept me alive. I'd seen enough of my own blood in the past two days that I never wanted to see it again.

"Troublesome food." His anger was not white-hot, as it had been with his thrall, it was arctic cold. It was subzero. His face had frozen into an expression of such rage I was sure he was going to reach over and snap my neck right off of my shoulders. Instead, he pulled the blade out. The tip of it, the part that had been lodged in his chest, was clean, but my blood lay on the length, thin and red and beading up slowly, like tears on the steel.

His tongue came out and licked the blade with a

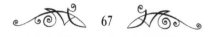

slow sensual motion that made my belly flop loosely. His eyes never left me, his expression suddenly back to that deadly neutral look. As though he felt nothing. I knew that wasn't true, but it unsettled me all the same.

"You obviously don't want to eat," he said in a low but lethal tone. "I do, however, and see no reason why both of us should go hungry."

I screamed and thrashed, but his cold hands shoved me into the mattress. Hot, salty tears fell down my cheeks, and my feet kicked and flailed. One of his hands pinned me down between my breasts, and the other grabbed my bleeding hand by the wrist. I bucked my hips to try to throw him off, but he was too heavy. His face rippled and changed, becoming more monstrous. Fangs appeared, needle sharp over his lips.

Those fangs plunged roughly into my wrist, drawing deep from the large artery there.

Dizziness spun through me. I was so weak and tired that my body could not decipher at first what was happening. I could only feel the ice of his lips, and the hot flush of my blood rushing out of me. His jaw clenched around my flesh, and I could do nothing but stare in horror at the monster on top of me. My mouth opened in a silent cry. Darkness washed over me. I felt like I was drowning in fire. Nothing made sense as my mind spun, and I hardly felt his lips leave my skin except that my body jerked in an automatic reaction, a whimper of relief torn involuntarily from my throat. I fell back onto the pillows, wilted, and drifted into black nothingness.

7

woke up the next morning to the sight of my bandaged hand and wrist on the pillow beside me, the curtains tightly closed, and Owen in a chair near my bed.

He looked tired and drawn. He rubbed his forehead with his long fingers, and his eyebrows were low over his eyes. It was so different to his normal, cold composure that I watched him, stunned, feeling like I was looking at an entirely different person. Not the monster I still wanted to plunge a knife into the heart of, but someone more human.

He caught sight of me staring at him and shifted awkwardly. Reaching out, he lifted my head slightly to put a glass of sweet milk to my lips. I swallowed it, then he laid my head back down with a tenderness

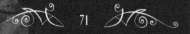

I would never have believed him capable of. It felt different this time. Not just being careful not to damage something prized. It was actual caring, or maybe even guilt. I could see it in the wrinkle of his brow and softness in his gaze. Somehow, something had changed. Like that flicker of hesitation I saw once before.

There was a vulnerability in his voice when he said, "I'm sorry if I hurt you. I don't usually react so violently."

Who the hell is he kidding? He's a vampire. He lives off violence.

I bit down my retort. I didn't really want to make him angry again.

I lifted my bandaged hand, holding it up in front of him as evidence. "You did hurt me. Look what you've done to me in just two days. How do you expect me to survive this?"

He shifted in his chair, turning away from my wounds on display. "I'm sorry. I will be more careful."

"I don't want you to be careful. I want you to let me go! Keeping me here like this, it's inhuman." *Of course it is, you idiot. He's not human.* But he did seem more human now than any other time we'd interacted. There was an almost palpable guilt coming from him. Maybe there was something of a man inside him after all. Maybe I could reach that, make him see me as more than just food. That was my only hope.

I stretched out, taking his hands into my fingers. He turned troubled eyes to meet mine, and I spoke as pleadingly and sincerely as I could. "I don't want to die."

He shook his head, releasing his fingers from my grasp. "All humans die."

"Okay, let me rephrase that. I don't want to die *imminently*." I couldn't keep the bitter tightness out of my voice.

"I will keep you alive as long as possible." The words were like a tender promise and he shook his head again, this time as though trying to clear it. He rubbed his fingers down his temples and schooled his expression back to neutral. He was clamming up, shutting down. The opportunity to connect with him was slipping through my fingers before I'd had the chance to do anything useful with it.

I decided to push harder. "Gee, thanks. That's not what I mean, and you know it. I want to go home. Being kept here, like this, is as good as death. Do you not see how cruel this is? Keeping me here, so you can nibble at me until I'm all dried up?"

"Do you enjoy crab legs?" He was looking down at his hands, laced tightly together in his lap.

The question caught me off guard. "Yes, I love them. Why?"

"Do you consider it fair to yank a crab from its

home, tear off one leg and toss it back?"

"I've never—"

"They harvest stone crabs one leg at a time. The leg grows back, but each time that crab is caught again its leg is taken. Is that humane behavior?" He finally glanced up at me, and his face was cold. Something moved in his eyes, as though the darkness there had lightened unperceptively.

Was he using this comparison to convince me, or himself?

Either way, I'll never eat crabs again, I swear it. I needed to change tack. "You used to be a human. Can't you remember what it's like?"

"It was a very long time ago." He settled back in his chair and tugged at the cuffs of his shirt.

"How old are you?" I asked, looking from his lean and elegant fingers to the wrinkle-free skin around his eyes. He didn't look like he'd hit thirty. I wasn't even sure why I was asking. Grasping at straws I suppose, keeping him talking in the hope I could find something to use, some leverage for my freedom. A way to show some kind of connection between us. Anything to make us equals. You don't feed on equals. Right?

"I have not been human for four hundred and thirty-one years."

I choked. Four hundred and thirty-one years? That was older than … well, older than the Constitution.

My grasp on history had never been very good, and I left the comparison at that. I struggled for another question to keep the conversation going. He wasn't much of a talker, though he seemed to be answering my questions easily enough. "Why did you become a vampire? Were you afraid of dying?"

"I do not fear death." He looked at me, strangely defiant, as though I were challenging him. "Nor have I ever feared it."

"But I do. Can you not understand that? Can't you just let me go?"

Something flashed across his eyes. "No. If you were anyone else, if you had any other blood, you would be home already. Normally I feed, then make the human forget before releasing them. I have never kept anyone this long before. It's far too risky, the chance of being discovered. But your blood is too delicious. I cannot let you go." He ran a hand over his hair, no longer perfectly slicked back but falling in a tousled mess. "I don't even understand it. It is as though I am mad for the taste of you."

"Please!" I begged. Even now, when we could almost have a conversation like real people, I wasn't getting anywhere, and desperation broke over me like a cold sweat. "Do that, please. Brain wipe me and drop me off on some corner. There are probably people out looking for me. Lots of people." *No one. No one would be looking for me, except for debt collectors.*

I didn't need to force tears for this scene.

"I'm sorry." As soon as the words left his mouth a confused expression crossed his face, then the anger slammed back over his features like a lid. "This is wrong. There's something about you, having you here … Stop speaking to me. I will not apologize to my food. I should not have to."

"I'm not food." I threw myself at him, grasping at his shirt. "I'm a person! Please! I'm a person! My name is Kitty French. I'm an actress who lives in West Hollywood. I live with ten people and I can barely pay—"

He wrapped his hands around my forearms, halting my assault. The grip was almost bruising and it made me stumble on my words, interrupting myself as I hissed at the sudden, dull pain. A dark and troubled expression traveled his chiseled face.

With a grunt, he set me free, his expression pained as he paced the side of the bed. He ran his hands up over his hair, mussing it, and seemed to be fighting a battle in his own mind. He was a completely different person to the cold monster from the day before. What had changed?

He'd fed.

Between the undead monster who'd tended to his strawberry with detached precision, to the man before me now, struggling with his emotions, he'd fed.

Maybe having a good drink of human blood left

him warmer, more human himself. A little less monstrous, but definitely more troubled. Maybe my blood really was sending him mad. That didn't sound like a fun result.

"This isn't good for you, keeping me here," I said. "It can't end well, for either of us."

His eyes met mine, and there almost seemed to be a slight shimmer of color in them before they turned dark again. There was something in his expression that ignited a shiver of undeniable attraction within me.

Ugh. No! I refused the feeling. I didn't care how beautiful he was, he was a *monster*. But looking at him right now, the monster barely seemed present.

"Please," I said.

"I ... can't." With a confused and angry look, he vanished.

Screw this shit. I was quickly going to go insane trying to judge the emotions and motives of my captor. I had to get out of here with no one's help but my own. The chain rattled and shook as I strained against it. I was sitting on the floor with my feet against the wall and pushing as hard as I could. My back ached and sweat rolled down my body, drenching my costume, but the bed posts held and the chain was still in place.

The door opened and the thrall came in, the same madhouse stare and smile on her face. I waved at her but she didn't seem to notice me. Instead, she

set the tray that held my breakfast on the dressing table then stripped the sheets off the bed.

I couldn't help but wonder if she would have made the bed with me in it. The way she tossed the sheets on and tucked them in made me think of the Stepford wives, only she was a hell of a lot less well-kept. I cringed a little at the sight of her handling the sheets. Her nails were long and cracked, black with grime.

Her eyes were vacant when I looked into them, the wheel was still turning but the hamster was dead. I waved a hand in front of her face and she didn't even blink. Pity welled up inside me. Had she once also been his meal plan? Blueberry, maybe?

Owen said he'd never kept food as long as he's kept me, so this woman was different somehow.

I shuddered all over. I would rather be dead than be a senseless ... thing.

That thought made me remember just how much I did *not* want to be dead, and how little I trusted the vampire to keep me alive.

Despondent, I sat on the bed and looked over at the breakfast tray. Tea slopped out of a pot, and there was a small saucer but no food on it. Maybe the maid was feeling the same strain I was in captivity and rebelling in small ways. Too bad it meant going hungry for me. I wondered if I should say something next time Owen came. I wanted to, to make sure I didn't go hungry, but at the same time, I didn't want the woman to be punished.

I followed her path out to the banister, peering down the stairs until she vanished through a door that gave me a glimpse of the kitchen. I yearned to follow her, partly for the freedom it offered and partly because of the food I dreamed was there. A few bits of steak and a glass of milk wasn't enough to keep me from starvation. With a sigh, I headed to the bathroom. I stared gloomily at myself in the mirror for a while, denied the bathtub's lure again, then decided to go back to bed. In the bedroom, a glint of silver caught my eye. There on the nightstand was the silver domed tray from last night. I swore I didn't remember it there before I walked out of the room. *Did crazy-clown lady bring this in? What is going on?*

I approached it as if it were a trap, checking on all sides before I slowly lifted the lid. Inside was the partly eaten meal, the steak already cut into tiny bites. The only silverware was a spoon, but I didn't care. With careful discipline, I devoured every bite and savored each flavor. I decided in that moment that I would never turn down a meal from Owen again. I'd relish every meal like it was my last. I might never know when it would be.

SELINA A. FENECH

8

Two nights passed. Owen didn't return. I hung there in that bedroom in a suspended state. My body gradually began to heal. The thrall brought me nearly endless pots of tea, but food was random and sporadic, only enough to nibble on. I hadn't had a proper meal since the truffle steak. I tried to talk to her, get her attention, but she just skulked in and out, creepy as all hell. The one time she actually looked at me, even briefly, I thought she was going to beat me to death rather than help me escape. There was something wild in her eyes, underneath the glassiness of Owen's hypnotism, that disturbed me to my core. I came to believe that she really had gone mad under his control. Pure human insanity scared me, maybe even more than Owen himself did.

I had nothing for company but the books on the shelves. They were a mixed bag of archaic philosophy, history texts, and long dead poets, but they were better than nothing. On and off I kept trying to plan an escape, but no new weapons miraculously emerged and the chain remained strong. So, I spent my days with Neitzsche, Descartes, Poe, and Shakespeare, and the nights standing at the full length of my leash, staring out over the ocean through the French doors.

At dusk on the third night, Owen finally came back. Tired of being alone, I was almost happy to see him. I set the book of old poetry on the bedside table, briefly considering trying to brain him with it. I figured the book wasn't that heavy and would probably be less effective than my attempt with the steak knife.

Then he approached. His face was cold and still, remote as the moon that hung in the corner of the open doors of the balcony. Any hint of humanity that was there when I'd seen him last was gone. This was all monster.

My body reacted to him again like he was the predator and I was prey, filling me with warning cries of, *Oh shit. He's going to kill me.* A cool trickle of fear ran through my belly.

Owen gave me a distasteful look, then disappeared briefly into the bathroom before returning. The closer he got to me, the more his face twisted with disgust.

unLife

I remembered the way he had softened when he drank from me last, and was almost desperate to get him to bite me again. I didn't know why that was, but it made some kind of sense. Even the best of us gets grouchy when hungry. And it had been two days since he last fed. I wanted him to change from this dead monster into the almost human man I could talk to, that I had a chance of reaching. *I have to keep him on my side, try to get in control of him or his emotions.*

"Been a while," I said. "You must be hungry." *Oh, gee, that was really subtle.* I should have just tilted my head and said, *here vampire, have a suck.*

He didn't seem to notice my slip up. "I am. But you are filthy. Why have you not bathed?"

I wouldn't. Not until I was free. It was the small pact I'd made with myself. There was too much temptation here, luring me to give in and stay, live in luxury and be fed exquisite food—when that food actually arrived—at the not-so-small price of giving up my personhood and being food myself.

I deflected. "Why haven't you been around? Your nutty maid has been all but starving me." I hadn't meant to bring her into this, but hunger and fear made me careless. I didn't want her punished, or for him to put her under more scrutiny if she was managing to break free.

Owen frowned, but there was no caring in the

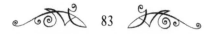

expression, just more distaste. "She has been strangely disobedient lately. I don't know why. I will see that you receive adequate food from now on. Now, I require *my* food to be clean."

In a swift movement, he uncuffed me and hauled me to my feet.

Instinct kicked in. I flailed my arms, hitting him in his sharp and straight nose. He seemed shocked by the blow and dropped me. There was a small bit of satisfaction in that, but even more satisfying was my run across the floor. My fingers reached for the doorknob, but before I could turn it his muscular arms wound around my waist, and he lifted me from the floor. My legs kept going, feet running nowhere as I was hauled backwards.

I screamed every curse word I had ever heard and even made a few up. I beat at his hands and arms, kicked his shins, and head butted him, which made me see stars but didn't seem to faze him at all.

I was too busy screaming and fighting to notice where we were going, until he dropped me in the middle of the bathtub. Water splashed up around me and slammed, wave-like, across the floor. My screams stopped, cutting off as abruptly as an air siren.

The tub was so deep my chest was submerged. I rubbed my aching ass cheeks, shooting Owen a nasty glare. The sodden gown billowed out around me, and the clotted and crusted blood on the front came loose in tiny, dark burgundy threads. Owen grabbed the corset and tore it from my body easily, as though it were wet tissue. I gasped and slipped in the water, managing to dunk myself again.

When I sat up, my drenched hair shedding water across my face, I screamed, "Are you trying to drown me?"

"Bathe." His voice held command.

The chemise remained on me, covering me a little, but it swirled and floated, the thin fabric's transparency accentuated by being wet. I still had a strapless bra and panties on underneath, but they were also thin and lacey. I curled forward, pulling my knees up to cover myself. "What if I don't want to?"

"Then I will make you."

The fuck you will. I'm normally an easygoing person. Hell, I've never really had much of a stomach for confrontation. When I told my folks I wanted to move to LA to become an actress, the uproar was so great I simply waited until they were asleep one night, then packed my stuff and left town. I wrote them a note. It wasn't like I ran away. I was twenty-one when I drove off from home. I didn't talk to them for a few weeks, until they had calmed down, just because I couldn't stand to fight with them. Even now, years later, we didn't talk much. I don't think Dad ever forgave me.

That's been my pattern my whole life. I hate to

fight and usually run from one. The only thing I had ever *really* fought for was my career. Or was it? I could see now how that wasn't true. I had been a coward, settling for parts I knew were no good. I had chosen a low-rent agent, who had trotted me out to a game that had landed me here, in the house of a vampire, because I was afraid to try for a better one.

I looked back at my career and wanted to laugh and cry. I had come to LA with such high hopes. I wanted to be rich and famous in a career I loved. I had found acting through a summer camp my parents had sent me on. There were always openings for the plays they put on every year, and I was in almost every single one of them. In acting I could be the person I always wanted to be, could be anyone else but myself. It was my escape route.

I had thought it would take me right out of my mundane little life, and it seemed like that dream would come true, at least. I had been taken out of my life in a way I'd never expected, with a high chance of losing it on a more permanent basis.

Rebellion surged inside me. Rebellion and a reserve of courage I had never known I had. I was going to fight him, and I was going to get out of here alive, period. I was not willing to die politely for him, or anyone else. I had dreams and plans and a life to live.

"I'd prefer to remain a stinking, filth-covered animal than wash for a fucking monster like *you*."

unlife

"Bathe," he said again. His eyes dilated, his fangs grew, and a shiver of force washed over me. My mind clouded, and terror iced my veins. Then it cleared just as quickly, replaced with anger.

"Fuuuck. Youuu," I replied, dragging out the words.

He seemed taken aback. Had he tried to compel me? Control me with his vampire will? If so, it hadn't worked. *Take that, one point to Kitty!*

His eyes narrowed. "Fine. Then I will bathe you." Owen's cold hands shot toward me. I gawped at him, all my thoughts of fighting him gone as he dipped a soft washcloth into the water, lathered a bar of sweet-smelling soap into it, and began to wash me.

Foamy circles bloomed on my shoulders and arms. I tried to squirm away from him, but his grip was tight and the tub too slippery. He unwrapped the sodden bandages on my hand and neck. He wiped tenderly around my wounds, clearing away more dried blood before washing my back with a strong, massaging motion.

I continued swearing at him, trying to argue with him, but he was completely non-responsive.

He washed my hair and I stared at him, trying to force him to look me in the eyes and really see me, as he gently wiped my chin, cheeks and lips. He just continued about his work, like a kitchen hand thoroughly rinsing every speck of dust from the corrugations of a lettuce leaf. I huddled over, my cleaned hair hanging like dark threads in the water, trembling with anger. I felt so powerless.

I could have taken over and at least washed myself, taken that control, but it felt too much like being obedient. Making myself be clean food for him. At least this way he had to work for it.

Once I was washed, he hauled me out of the tub effortlessly. The loose-fitting chemise hung wet and heavy, clinging to me in a way that left nothing to the imagination. He approached me with a towel, and I pushed him away, snatching the towel off him. It was done. I was all washed up. I didn't need to have him drying me, too. I held the towel up between us and shimmied my shoulders until the saturated gown slipped off and squelched on the floor. Then I wrapped myself, wet underwear and all, in the warm, fluffy fabric, taking a second offered towel for my hair. I didn't have the energy or will to dry it, so I just wrapped it loosely.

I felt wilted as Owen led me back to bed and returned the shackle to my wrist. Drowsy and flooded with emotions. I had lost that round. It was clear the futility of fighting him when he was like this. I would gain no ground until he fed.

The satin sheets were slick and chilled, and I curled up into them, wanting only to cry myself to sleep, but he rolled me onto my back.

The mattress sagged beneath his weight as he

bent down on top of me. I tilted my head, revealing the undamaged side of my neck, and whispered, "Do it. Take my blood, Vampire."

His teeth grazed my neck then went lower, hovering below my collar bone.

When his teeth sunk deep into me, I barely felt the pain, but I couldn't stop the soft and involuntary cry that came from my mouth.

His weight hovered over me then came down. I shivered at the cold radiating from his skin, and my fingers curled into fists. I knew he had to bite me because it made him more human, but self-preservation, instinct, and hatred won over. I raised fists to hit him, but my hands fell to the mattress as he gripped them tightly in his own, holding them captive. His body pressed along the length of mine, and while I knew it was to hold me still, I couldn't help but writhe, feeling the heat rising in me to drive off the chill that came from him.

I could feel my blood flowing into him, strengthening him. I looked down. His dark head was just above my breast, and his powerful mouth brought tiny trails of blood welling up.

His body warmed, and one of his hands moved, tracing gently up my arm. My breath caught sharply in my throat.

Then it was over.

His teeth withdrew but his firm and heavy body

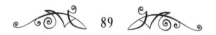

was still on top of mine. Owen looked at me with a deep frown, then traced the bruises on my neck with a finger. I already knew that my newest bite would not bruise the same way. It had felt different, gentler, if that was possible. Was I getting used to it, or was he being more careful?

Owen was so close I felt his cold, lifeless breath against my skin when he spoke. "I was too hasty. I thought you were merely a sweet meal when I first bit you, and once I started, once I truly tasted you, it was almost impossible to stop. I hurt you more than I should have, and for that, I'm sorry."

His voice was so achingly low, creeping into the deepest parts of my body. There was almost a tremble in it, the same confused, troubled tone he'd had after the last time he'd fed. Feeding really was what changed him. The man here with me now wasn't the same monster that had just bathed me like a damned vegetable.

I sought out his gaze and held it. The black of his eyes had also lightened slightly again, and there was the tint of some other undiscernible color. *Please, let me reach him.* "You hurt me more every minute you keep me captive."

A small growl emerged from his throat and he moved until his heartbreaker of a face was inches above mine. "This pleading has to end. There will be no more conversations between us, no more heart-to-heart talks. I do not have to keep you from feeling fear or treat you kindly. I will not apologize to you, and I will treat you as I see fit. You are food, nothing more."

His voice caught, and he seemed to force the words out. His eyes were filled with an uncertainty that didn't match what he was saying. As though he was trying to win a debate on a topic he didn't believe in.

And I want to win this round. I reached up, trailing my hand down his cold cheek, hoping for him to feel the warmth of my touch, to feel me as human.

I whispered, "Nothing more?"

His gaze flicked over my face, and his mouth parted, then he turned away, looking deeply confused.

I bit my lip, my eyelids lowering as I tried to determine what that confusion meant. Had I finally gotten through to him? No. That was different. That look had almost seemed lustful, and not just for blood.

My chest tightened beneath the fluffy towel, and my mind raced.

Maybe he is seeing me as something more.

I could use that. If he was feeling something, anything for me, I had to keep trying. It's not like I hadn't acted my way through sex scenes before. I'd do anything in order to get out of there.

He shifted, lifting his weight off me, and I was worried he was simply going to up and leave. There

seemed to be no other way around it. I had to get his attention, and fast.

I propped myself up on one elbow and pressed my lips to his. There was a risk that I'd read him wrong, that he'd simply rebuff me. But he didn't.

He paused for a moment, then kissed me back.

Our mouths pressed against each other; hot meeting cold. His tongue slid against mine, tasting of blood. There was desperation in his touch, his chilled fingertips running over my arms, leaving burning trails behind them. A soft growl came from his throat.

He wants me. Not just my blood, not just as food. He wants me.

The idea thrilled me more than it should have. It was power. It was opportunity. It was also disturbing, the way my body responded in return.

I'm acting, I told myself firmly, ignoring the low ache of desire that built within me.

I tugged at his shirt, releasing buttons as his shoulders rolled above me. The firm waves of his chest muscles delighted my fingers. He was sculpted, but only his temperature reminded me of stone. His skin gave under the press of my fingers. His muscles twitched and rippled under my touch like a true human lover.

Owen's hand drifted down my body, loosening the towel around me, and coming to rest in a strong grip on my thigh. I moaned and shuddered with need.

I thrust a hand to the fly of his black jeans. The handcuff scraped against his abs and rattled loudly. We both paused. I jerked my hand again, making a show of how the restraints kept my hand from reaching that bit farther, even though the chain was simply tangled beneath us. *Release me*, I begged with my eyes.

Owen's gaze went from heavy to wide-eyed. His body went rigid and he got off me.

He was two feet away in a flash, his brows knitted and lips twitching. "You … you were seducing me in an attempt to escape?"

You couldn't blame a girl for trying, could you? It seemed he could though, so I said nothing. His hands clenched and unclenched, and he paced, shooting me wild glares. He was furious and it showed.

"I do not know why you make me feel as you do, Strawberry, how you leave me so … confused. I've half a mind to kill you now and be done with it."

Scared shitless doesn't begin to describe how I was feeling. Then I remembered something, he was just as much a foodie as I was, but in a different way. He would savor my succulent blood until he could not get any more flavor or enjoyment from me, whether he liked it or not. Or whether I did either. A gourmand wouldn't light their favorite restaurant on fire just because the veal got a bit frisky with them.

"Go on, then. Kill me now, Vampire. Do it," I challenged.

He left, slamming the door so hard that books tumbled off the bookshelf. Making him angry was a bad mistake. If he ignored me for a day or two, he might come back all undead and unemotional, and kill me for the hell of it. He might decide I was like that trendy restaurant with the great food but the bad wait times and sloppy service. He might not think me worth it anymore.

I might have to rethink my strategy. Or rethink whether it was still a strategy, or just an excuse to let my body have its way. Was I really attracted to him? That monster? No. That was a hard no.

But when he was different, more human ... I had to admit, there was something there. He was still the man who had kidnapped and hurt me, who would probably kill me. *Is this what Stockholm syndrome feels like?* I didn't know, but I did know it was taking the hot bad boy attraction thing to a whole new level. I pulled my towel up and rolled over to try to sleep. There was nothing more I could do now.

A quiet cackle at the balcony jerked my head up. The thrall met my stare with her normal grin, but her eyes were bloodshot and dangerous. They weren't vacant as usual. Instead, a sinister glee lingered in them. How long had she been standing there watching me? Watching me and Owen? I jerked the satin sheet up over my exposed body.

"Prrretty girrrl." The thrall's voice scraped from her throat in a long, slow whisper.

I clung to the sheet, scared out of my wits.

The maid backed away into the unlit hall, the glint from her teeth the last thing visible in the dark.

I collapsed onto the pillow, curling up on my side. I had to get out of this madhouse.

9

I woke up the next morning, tangled in the towel with only my underwear on. A quick visit to the bathroom confirmed the corset was ruined, and the chemise remained in a puddle on the floor. I hung it to dry for later, but for now I had access to no other clothes. The room was always a pleasant temperature, so I probably could have wandered around mostly nude, but I had some modesty left in me.

I considered tearing and tying a sheet together into an elaborate toga, but resorted to simply wrapping a new big fluffy bath towel around myself.

I was happy to have something on when the maid came in again.

She surprised me, showing up at a time outside of her regular routine, her eyes lit with something

not there before. She held a giant meat cleaver in one hand, and a raw whole chicken in the other. She was wearing the same ratty, dirty clothes. *Did she ever change?* Even from across the room the smell made me gag so I doubted it. The only upkeep she seemed to do on herself was to smear that bright red lipstick around her mouth in a horrific clown smile.

I don't think she saw me standing at the bathroom door, but I watched her like a petrified deer.

"Pretty girl," she crooned as she set the chicken down on the nightstand and began to cut it into bits and pieces. I kept still, hoping she wouldn't notice me and decide she wanted to chop me up as well. Terror rose in me, greater than the panic I'd felt when Owen had first sunk his fangs into me and left me fighting for my life.

The thrall kept chopping. Pieces of raw chicken flicked onto the wall. The mangled corpse minced smaller and smaller. Bones cracked. The cleaver dripped thin pink blood onto the carpet. The woman hummed a quiet song through whistling teeth. It was so bizarre, so surreal that hysteria bubbled up in my chest and I laughed silently. I covered my face with my hands to try to muffle the gasping breath I couldn't seem to control that was halfway between a sob and a giggle.

Tears welled up and I battled them back. I could not afford to cry. Tears were a luxury, and right then what I needed was a stronger, harder emotion, one that would shake me to the core and help me survive. I just couldn't seem to find it.

The chopping sound ceased. *Was she coming for me next?* If she killed me now, all it meant was Owen couldn't have me for supper.

No. At least with Owen, I still had time and the hope of escape.

I uncovered my eyes, preparing to defend myself, but the thrall stood vacant and eerie in the center of the room, staring at the ceiling. The sun picked out the grey streaks in her hair, and I realized how old she was. How many of her years had been lost in this twisted servitude? Terror of a new sort hit me. Was I going to wake up one morning, old and bent over and used up? Just how long would he keep me alive as his food? I had been thinking in terms of weeks, months, but what if it was years, or *decades*?

I suddenly felt an overwhelming surge of pity for the woman before me. Against the instincts clamoring in my head to stay quiet and hide, I edged into the bedroom.

I kept my voice soft and gentle. "Hey. What's your name?"

I don't know why I asked. I didn't really expect her to answer.

Time ticked by. I counted the seconds in the beats

of my heart.

A grotesque smile stretched its way across her painted lips, and she batted her eyelashes before saying, "Loretta." Her voice was lilting and sweet when she replied, girlish even.

Sorrow filled me. She still had a name. Perhaps she was a lot more like me than I cared to recognize. She was a prisoner here, too. Maybe more so, since her mind clearly wasn't as free as mine.

I moved closer, in slow, careful movements, circling around beside the bed. "I'm Kitty."

"Kitty ..."

"Yeah, that's right. Kitty."

She crooned, "Kitty, kitty, kitty. Meeeow."

I blinked at her. The reply was crazy talk, but at least I was getting replies. My mind raced with the possibilities. I could conceivably reach her, enlist her help in escaping. Both of us could escape.

"Loretta," I said softly, as she began to clean my room in her jerky autopilot manner. Except instead of a duster or cloth, she was using a chunk of chicken, smearing the severed neck across the top of the dresser and over the bookshelves. "Loretta, do you want to get out of here?"

"Get out. Out of heeere." The word was a drawn-out hiss of air. Green rot had set in along the upper edges of her teeth, turning her gums a speckled black. My stomach churned, but I couldn't let her see my disgust. I was reaching her. I knew it.

"Yes, wouldn't you like to go home, Loretta? Where are you from?"

"Get out, kitty kitty." Her eyes became cunning and her mouth twisted into the upside-down smile of an insane clown. "Kitty, kitty, meeeeeeeeow!"

"Yes, I'm Kitty." My optimism faded with every passing second. "You're Loretta. We're prisoners but we could both get free if you would help me." I could tell I was losing whatever ground I had won. Her eyes were glassy, but something wicked sparked inside them.

She barked like a dog, lunging at me and yipping loudly. I recoiled, her body odor hitting my nose like a stone wall. She slunk closer, her mouth opening and closing in huffing pants, her tongue hanging out almost to her chin. Drool dripped in silver strands down her chest.

I backed away and hit the bed, falling onto it. "Loretta, please, listen—"

She lunged at me. The crazy-assed creature thought I was a cat, and she was a dog! She pounced on the bed and I rolled off just in time. Her jaw snapped on the air where my nose had been a moment before.

I ran around the side of the bed. Loretta went straight over and caught up with me. Her teeth closed around my arm. "Get off!" I howled, beating at her head with my free hand. When she fell back,

I saw to my horror that she'd broken the skin. The impressions of her teeth on my arm welled with blood.

Loretta stumbled backward, her tongue lolling out and her eyes rolling madly like marbles in their sockets. She barked again and I ran for the bathroom. I got there just in time, slamming the door shut as far as it could go given the chain stuck in it. She howled and barked and giggled and shrieked. I could hear her feet pattering up and down in front of the door. The chain pulled taut as I strained to break free, wanting to put some solid wood between the two of us.

Her feet quit moving, but I could see her through the crack in the door. I pressed my back to it, bracing my feet on the toilet partition wall to keep her out. The door shuddered as she kicked and punched it.

"Stop it!" I screamed. "Stop!"

My cries seemed to enrage her. The blows landed harder, jarring my spine and sending bolts of pain through my legs and feet. It felt like she was throwing her whole body against it, and I could hear her long, cracked nails scraping at the wood. I grabbed towels and wedged them like doorstops under the door.

The bathroom window was the only other way out, but I wasn't going to get far while still cuffed, so it didn't seem worth it. Until Loretta began to hit the door so hard the wood split open under her blows. I ran for the window and attempted to open it. It was stuck, but after a few frantic moments of shoving at it the frame gave with a rusty screech, and the window flung outwards.

Cool air slapped me in the face. It was raining.

I hoisted myself up, balancing my stomach on the sill to look out. The drop was sheer and long, at least two stories, if not three. When Loretta burst through the door behind me, I didn't think about it, I just tumbled out. I tried to cling to the sill, to dangle from it out of reach until she left me alone, but it was slick with rain and my fingertips slipped.

For a split second, I was in free fall.

I reached the end of the chain and my body snapped in the air, sending pain shooting into every part of me. The chain swung me like a pendulum, and I grabbed it with my other hand, clinging for dear life. The towel I wore slipped loose and fluttered to the ground far below. The cold and the sharp jerk that nearly dislocated my shoulder left me gasping and blinking to try to clear the stars out of my vision.

Icy rain hit my nearly bare body, but terror chilled me more when I looked up at the maniac's face hanging out of the window, her hands hauling at the chain.

Part of me hoped the yanking would somehow sever my restraints. If only I could survive the fall … I glanced down again. It was so far up.

"Let me go, you psycho!" I yelled, digging my feet

into the side of the stucco walls. Blood bloomed against the rough side of the house as my toes scraped and found purchase then lost it again.

She let go. I dropped a few sickening feet and screamed like a banshee. Loretta opened her mouth and howled as well. She leaned out, her ratty hair creating a stinking nimbus around her slack face. She grinned wildly, gnashing her teeth as she continued to grunt and growl like some wild animal.

She angled farther and farther out, perching like a gargoyle in the window, her eyes searching for a way to grab me and bring me back in. Little trickles of pebble-filled sand fell past me, but I didn't comprehend the danger until there was a low groaning creak.

The windowsill gave under her weight. It shot past me, a chunk of it hitting me in the side of my head. Loretta never even screamed, she just went down, her witch-like hair standing up in a nearly comical peak, and her tongue still hanging from her chapped, raw lips.

She hit the fence with an explosive crack, then smacked onto the concrete of the tennis courts. Shards of thick wood lay scattered about her bloodied and broken body. The green of the court was marred by a spreading maroon pool. She didn't move.

I buried my face into the wall. The rain could not wash away the tears that fell from my eyes. There was no way to survive that fall.

My wrist ached. I was sure it would break, or my hand would just tear free from my arm. My other hand grew slick with blood, trying to haul myself up time and again, slipping away from the chain and causing me to drop sharply each time, my weight causing fresh agony in my bound arm and wrist. The rain chilled my skin, and the wind blew into my eyes, forcing me to close them. I couldn't stop shaking.

10

Twilight hovered over the world.

Owen's face appeared out the broken window. He quickly surveyed the scene, and I thought he would reel me in like a fish on a line. Instead, he jumped out of the window as well.

He held what remained of the sill with one hand, and brought me in to him with his other, tucking me against his shoulder. He was cold, but for once, I was colder, and clung to his dry clothes desperately for warmth.

With the ease of something like flight, he lifted us both back inside.

When my feet touched firm ground again, my legs gave away underneath me, but Owen kept me upright. All of my limbs were shaking, and my head felt like it was about to detach from my body. The arm I'd hung from had no feeling left in it at all.

Owen scooped my legs up and cradled me as he stepped into the shower and ran the hot water. He wore a fine silk shirt, suit pants, and leather shoes, but didn't seem to care. He stood with me under the water, letting it drip warmth back into my body.

He undid the manacle from my tortured wrist, and I wasn't surprised when he simply moved it to my ankle. He started gently massaging the life back into my fingers.

Even though he hadn't fed since the night before, there was still some hint of humanity in him. His face had gone the color of milk—deathly pale, but with a slightly cream cast, rather than the purer white it had been. Water beaded and dripped from his long lashes, making them cling together, star-like.

"Tell me what happened," he said in a soft voice.

My teeth chattered around my words. "Your nuthouse slave attacked a chicken."

"I saw."

"Then tried to eat me."

Owen glanced at my arm, where her round, blunt teeth had left a semi-circular mark

"I'm sorry. I had no idea she'd become so free from my control." That concept seemed to trouble him deeply.

It troubled me more.

"It was probably your control that sent her insane. Keeping her brain numb, making her serve you. It was worse than being a prisoner."

Owen gave me a level look. "You would not pity her if you knew who she really was. She was one of my employees until I first realized the psychopath she was. She had killed at least three husbands and two of my waitresses before I turned her into my thrall."

In death her face had been calm and still, wiped clean. She looked like an aged woman at peace. Was she really a murderer? I recalled the gleeful way she had chopped up the chicken's carcass, the way she'd hunted me, and looked back at him. "Why didn't you let her just stand trial?"

"Do you really think that is the only justice in this world?" He snorted, and I saw his lips curl in disgust. "Do you think I didn't try that first?"

I didn't have an answer to that one.

"Things are rarely that simple, Strawberry. She was a dangerous woman, her mind lost to violent illness before I took her in. There is no need to pity her in life or death. When the justice of your kind failed, I decided I could not allow her to roam free."

Tears gathered in my eyes, then fell and splattered his chest. "But it was my fault. I tried to talk to her, tried to run away. I made her snap. I killed Loretta."

"Loretta killed herself." The words were mild. His

arms tightened almost imperceptibly around me.

I squeezed my eyes shut, but tears pushed out insistently anyway. "She didn't have to. Why didn't you just let her go?" I yelled, angry with him for no reason at all, or maybe for every reason.

"Would you rather her be free to torment innocents?"

"Why didn't you just kill her then?" I was hysterical, but I couldn't seem to stop the angry, bitter words.

He paused for a long moment. "It gets lonely."

The words opened my soul, cut me to the already raw core of my being. It got lonely in this isolated, windswept little spot of earth. In the long years that made up the centuries. In the dark hours of night without seeing the day.

He was lonely.

I whispered, barely audible over the sound of the shower running around us, "That still gives you no right to hold people against their will."

Owen set me down on my feet.

"Do you hate me so much, Strawberry?"

My feelings for him were incredibly conflicted. On one hand, I had begun to care about this side of him in ways that would have seemed unimaginable to me a few days ago, but on the other, I longed to be free of his teeth inside my flesh, and to be able to walk in the sunlight unencumbered by fear.

I dropped my head. "I hate the monster you can be."

Owen turned the shower off and carefully dried

me. He wrapped me in a warm towel, then left the bathroom without a word. I didn't move, except to sit on the edge of the bathtub. I wasn't sure my legs would support me yet, and my abraded toes stung. I felt so incredibly tired.

It was some time before he came back. He returned in dry pants, bare feet, and still buttoning up a new shirt. The moonlight filtered through the windows, outlining his incredible body and handsome face. The bloodsucking thing had kidnapped me, but he was undeniably gorgeous. He picked me up and carried me out to the bedroom. I didn't try to resist.

The bedroom was spotless, cleared of any chicken remains and mess from my struggle. I looked around, amazed at how fast Owen could be when he wanted to.

I caught him staring lustfully at the pulse in my neck.

He must have noticed. "I won't feed on you after all you've been through. You need to recover."

"No. You should drink. I want you to. I like you better after you've eaten." I didn't bother anymore with games or tricks. My cards were on the table.

I sat on the edge of the bed.

Owen stood close in front of me, and I almost reached up to feel the lines of his stomach muscles I'd just seen under his shirt.

Then he knelt between my knees. His fingers traced my neck, where he'd bit below my collar bone,

and then the bite on my wrist. I held my breath, and the uncontrollable shivering I'd just recovered from struck again.

He took both of my hands in his, staring again at the damage the handcuff had done, then gently lifted my other hand to his mouth. His lips touched softly against my palm before moving to my wrist, just below the other bite mark.

I barely felt his teeth go in, just the hot rush of blood flowing between us. I swooned, and he caught me around the waist, pulling me tight against his chest, my legs wrapped either side of where he still knelt at the edge of the bed.

With my legs wrapped around him, and his arm wrapped around me, he stood up, lifting us, still clutching my wrist to his mouth and drinking. A confused rush of desire blazed through me, and I leaned into him, pressing my cheek to his neck.

He bent forward, laying me on the bed with him on top of me. His chest pressed down over mine gently. I felt a sudden, strong yearning for him to be closer. The pounding of blood rushing through me, and a blur of emotions, left me panting. My body moved of its own instinct, my hips pressing up toward his.

Owen pulled his teeth from my wrist, kissing away the blood.

When he rolled off me and sat up, I tried to hide my disappointment.

"I hope I didn't take too much. I worry about your health," he said.

I probably looked more feverish than ever. "Nah, I'm fine. I hope you, you know, had enough to eat."

He smiled. It didn't reach his worried eyes, but it was still a smile. I didn't realize that was possible. I gaped up at him in surprise. He looked ... normal. Like a person instead of an undead killer. His face had color, and his eyes had expression. His skin had gone a beautiful warm ivory, but when I reached for his arm his flesh still felt cool beneath my fingers.

His hand stroked my hair tenderly, and I turned my cheek into his palm, seeking comfort even though he was the reason I needed it.

Too many complex emotions struggled to unleash themselves from inside me. Abruptly, I remembered writhing against him in a stupor of passion and blushed so hard my face felt like someone had held a blowtorch to it.

"Soooo," I finally said, making the awkward silence more awkward.

"This is so odd."

I blinked then said, "Yeah, being held against my will by a vampire who is trying to kill me slowly is certainly not anything I would've put in my yearbook as a future plan. But calling it 'odd' feels a bit understated, to be honest."

He chuckled and shook his head, his still damp

hair falling over his eyes. "You are doing something to me, Strawberry. I am feeling things I have not felt in centuries. I've never had blood like yours before. I've never been so ... warm. I'm not sure I like it. It's as though when I drink from you, I become weakened somehow."

"Maybe you should let me go then," I suggested. "Keep us both happy."

My attempt at humor fell flat. His lips thinned to a line, and his shoulders sagged.

"Look, my blood probably just tastes good because I like eating nice things. Bring in any old vampire groupie and feed them that fancy food you've been giving me, and you'd probably get the same result. You don't need me."

"No, there is something uniquely special about you." It almost sounded like an apology.

His fingers weren't as cool as usual as they reached out and touched mine. I shivered at the disconcerting sensation of him feeling so human. Dawn brightened the windows, rosy little hints of light barely cracking across the uppermost edges.

Owen noticed too and stood up from the bed. How had the night passed so quickly? I remembered the stories of *Arabian Nights*, how Scheherazade stayed alive by telling the bloodthirsty sultan stories he couldn't resist. I wasn't sure what I could tell Owen that would keep me on his good side longer, so I asked him a question instead.

"Do you miss daylight?"

"I can still see sunlight, from a safe distance. I will sometimes brave it, for the right sunrise. It makes me weak though."

"Is it worth it?"

"Most things that make us weak are." His lips twitched.

A confusing realization settled heavily over me. I hated that he took my blood, battened on me like a leech, but I liked the person he became afterwards. Genuinely *liked* him.

I tried to swallow that feeling away and focus on the monster side of him. "How did you turn into a vampire? Is it like on TV? How does it happen?"

He eyed me seriously. "I won't make you a vampire, if that is what you are angling for."

"Oh darn," I retorted in as sarcastic a voice as I could muster. "What a shame, I would love to give up eating crème brulee in favor of a little O neg."

Owen smiled almost wistfully, then tucked me into the warm covers of the bed. The fluffed-up pillows and thick comforter were like heaven compared to the rough side of the building lashed with rain. I nestled into them, my eyelids growing heavy. Owen sat down above the covers. As he settled in next to me, I couldn't help but wonder what he had been like when he was alive.

That was dangerous thinking. I knew that it was. He was a vampire, purely and simply, and even though he looked human at times, he was not.

I probed again, regardless. "You didn't answer my question."

Owen looked at me. "Strawberry, you should not ask so many questions."

"If you're going to keep me here you might as well entertain me. Come on, Vampire, tell me a story." I said the words casually but under my skin my heart was racing. I loved a good story even if it was bound to have a pretty unhappy ending, which it was obvious my own was destined for.

Owen sat still for a while and I didn't think he was going to talk. Then slowly, quietly, he did. "I fell in love with a woman I thought I would die without. Instead, it happened that to be with her, I had to die."

"You became a vampire for love? Then why isn't Mrs. Vampire still around?"

"She died centuries ago."

Oh. Sympathy for him filled me, although I didn't want it to. "I'm sorry. I thought you vampires were immortal. How did she die?"

Owen moved off the bed and turned away. "I killed her."

What kind of guy killed the love of his life? Vampire guys. That's what he was. And I couldn't forget what my ultimate goal was. Escape.

UnLife

Dawn showed its full face in the glass of the doors. Thin streaks of gold lay on the carpet, and Owen turned back to me with a look of such heartbreak that I felt the pang deep in my own chest. One second he was standing there looking down at me, the next he was gone. I saw a blur in the corner of my eye, and heard the door open then close, but that was all.

I lay there, confused and wrung out. The sun rose above the horizon, followed by a band of clear blue sky that showed in the distance. Birds sang loudly, and I rolled over on my back.

"I really have to get out of here," I said to the ceiling, but it didn't bother answering.

SELINA A. FENECH

11

Time began to blend together. I found myself sleeping during the day more often and staying up with Owen at night. He would feed me then feed from me, coming in as a monster, and leaving as a man.

He was gentler now when he fed, and the newer bites didn't leave gory marks like his earlier ones did. But still, I felt my health waning slowly, as though every time he drank from me, a few days of my life were sucked away.

Having the cuff around my ankle instead of wrist made it a little more out of sight, out of mind, but I still regularly tested its strength. No new chances at escape emerged, and some days I almost gave up any hope of freedom in my future. My thoughts and emotions grew so conflicted my insides were at war.

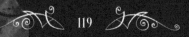

The emotions spilled out, making me a teary, giggly, snappy mess. Mood change extraordinaire, that was me. The fact that Owen, on the other hand, seemed to be growing more and more patient, caring, and sensitive in turn was strangely infuriating.

One night, Owen brought me a simple, but truly delicious, meal of handmade ravioli filled with whole egg yolks, coated in crispy sage and burnt butter sauce. He wandered out to the balcony, staring at the stars while I ate. When I finished, I followed him out, figuring it was his turn.

The long chemise from my costume I still wore hung off my shoulders and trailed behind me on the carpet.

Instead of biting me, Owen asked, "Do you swim?"

"Yes. Why?"

"Would you like to?"

"Uh, I guess?"

Without another word, he gathered me in his arms, released the shackle off my ankle, and leaped to the top rail of the balcony. I screamed. I wasn't sure if vampires could commit suicide by falling to their death and I didn't want to find out either. I *did* know I was very fragile and breakable even if he wasn't. We took flight. Terror had me in its grip and I screamed all the way down.

He landed featherlight on the concrete below.

"You still don't trust me," he said.

unlife

I was shocked that he could talk given that my arms were locked in a death grip around his neck. I could have killed him if he wasn't already dead.

"I trust you as much as a drunken frat boy, pulling stunts like that," I snapped.

With a troubled look, he placed me gently onto my feet. It struck me how different he had become. His flashes of coldness still happened, but he rarely seemed inhuman.

"Go, swim. Enjoy some exercise." He nodded toward the water.

There was an exit gate to the side. I stared at it for a moment, knowing there was no way I could outrun Owen. With a sigh, I turned my attention to the pool.

The naturalistic style of it was stunning, and I couldn't resist wading slowly in. The chemise spread around me like a cloud, and I enjoyed the way it moved in the water, but it tangled too much around my limbs to allow me to swim. I ducked under the water and slipped it off. I felt a little self-conscious in my lacy underwear in front of Owen, but the water was dark, cozy, and concealing. My black hair hung down long, swirling around my chest, and the waterfall played a soft tune as it dripped and dropped at the other end of the pool.

The water was blood warm, the moon above sent spangles across the tiny little wavelets created by

121

my movements. The flowers planted around the pool gave off a heavenly smell of rose and jasmine.

I plunged under, gliding through a few leisurely laps, then swam over to the side where Owen sat, watching me silently. I folded my arms on the edge.

The vitality of being immersed in water in this dreamlike setting left my philosophical.

"How do you see the world? Is it different to when you were human?" I asked.

"As a vampire, your senses and emotions become different. Some are stronger, and some fade away entirely ... But it's been so long I can hardly remember. How do you see it?"

I stared around me. Everything was sharp and angular, black and gray with occasional splashes of color. The roses were scarlet but the dark shadows behind them made the blood red of them seem even brighter, arterial even.

The sky was an immense dark bowl with bright pinpricks of stars, and the moon hung wafer thin and bright in one corner. The mountain was cloaked by darkness, making its edges softer, kinder.

I described what I saw in halting tones. I was used to reciting other people's lines, not putting my own thoughts into words. It was a strange feeling that left me unsure and self-conscious. He sat on the lounge chair, leaning forward to listen, elbows on his thighs.

"No. I do not see the world the way you do. Maybe I never did."

He seemed softer tonight, less intense.

"Do you miss the day?"

"I can see sunlight from afar."

"I know, but do you miss it? I mean, being out in it and feeling it on your face, getting a tan, or hanging out at the beach, that kind of thing."

"I never really *hung out* at the beach." His tone was a bit sarcastic. "I do miss riding though."

"Riding? Like on a bike or something?"

"No, on horseback." He stared out into space. "I used to love to ride."

"Why don't you do it anymore? I mean, can't you ride a horse at night?"

"Animals tend to shy away from me now."

Oh. I had forgotten for a moment he was a monster. He seemed so human tonight. Pity filled me. I fought the sensation. He didn't deserve my pity. But his face was suffused with a kind of longing I had never seen on it before. I wasn't sure what to say, but he spoke, saving me from having to say anything.

"The first woman I fell in love with I met riding. Rather, I was riding, and her horse had spooked and was running away with her across Hyde Park."

A tiny smile ghosted across his lips. "Her hat had come off, and she had slung her leg across the horse in a decidedly unladylike manner, which hiked her skirts up almost to her thighs. Still, she managed to get the stallion under control."

A haunted kind of happiness crinkled the corners of Owen's eyes and he shook his head, staring across at the waterfall.

"She sounds like one hell of a horsewoman."

"She was a lot of things."

A coyote howled from somewhere and I flinched, a movement he saw though I hadn't thought he was paying attention at all.

"There's nothing to fear. They can't get past the walls."

Owen stirred again and sighed, a heavy sigh that sounded hurt and tired all at once.

"I wish time had not moved on so much."

"What do you mean?"

He laughed but there was no humor in it. "I mean, I don't know how to live in this time. It wasn't something I thought about before I was turned, that time would march on and leave me behind."

"Progress can be hard to adjust to," I agreed. "I guess most of us don't really notice it too much until we look back and think about it. My mom used to talk about the microwave, how she never had one growing up until she was a teenager because they just weren't around, or because they were too expensive. She barely uses hers now because she never got used to it. But for my generation, well, I can't imagine not having one."

Owen nodded. "Every time I think I adapt, something new comes along. Sometimes so fast it has
already passed to the next thing before I have had
a chance to catch up."

I swirled a slow three-sixty in the water, looking
at the vast mansion behind me, full of expensive
modern appliances. "You don't seem to be doing too
badly. Why did you turn vampified then, if it's so
hard? I mean didn't you think about forever being
such a long time?"

For a minute I was sure he would tell me to mind
my own business but then he spoke, "At the time
being with her forever seemed like the proposition
of paradise and I had no idea of how little like that
it would be."

I didn't have to ask. I knew she was the girl on the
runaway horse. The woman he had at some point,
for some reason killed. The breeze ran across my
body. My hair dripped down my back and the scent
of chlorine grew stronger. I shivered.

"Adelle St. Delaurents. She was the daughter of
a duke and I was the second son of a mere baron,
an officer in the military whose entire pay went to
support myself in what was hardly a high style. The
match was impossible. Adelle's family already had
her betrothed to a very wealthy man when we met."

I gaped slightly. Talk of dukes and barons made

my head spin in a very not-in-Kansas-anymore kind of way. It was so far outside my field of experience, like something from a period romance, not something someone brought up in a conversation about their ex.

Owen continued, "She had to wed. Back then, women were little more than commodities, even the ones born into privilege had little or no control over their lives. A beautiful daughter was often sold off to the highest bidder. They were given huge wardrobes and trotted out to balls and fetes and soirees so they could have a chance to make the best match possible for their family. It was all done with little, if any, consideration to their heart or desires."

The bitterness that lay in his words stirred sympathy in me. The lack of freedom women of a past era suffered cut close to home, especially given my current situation. "Why didn't you two run off together?"

"To run away would have meant causing the ruination of her entire family. She married the man she was betrothed to. It drove me crazy. Her husband was thirty years older, and he was cruel. He found her too headstrong and outspoken, and he spared no mercy in his attempts to change her."

I shuddered. I could well imagine the methods he employed in his attempts at reeducating Adelle.

"We managed to see each other at times, but it was never enough. Soon, we got careless, and her husband became suspicious."

unLife

There was a lengthy pause. I did my best to wait it out but after a minute I couldn't stand it anymore. "You totally got her pregnant, right?"

"No. Regardless, he took her away to France for a year and my company went to India. When I came back, she was ill, close to death. She recovered slowly, but she was never the same."

I didn't ask what her illness was. Back then, even the common flu could be deadly. But also, part of me worried that if I knew, I'd care more, and I was doing my best not to care.

"She became terrified of dying. More, she was afraid of getting old. Adelle was well aware that her only commodities were her youth and her beauty. She had begun to take all sorts of weird little cures. I suppose in retrospect it was no odder than what people do now—facelifts, having botulism shots, and getting their skin sanded down—but at the time it seemed very strange. She would take these long baths in milk and roses. She coated her body in honey and had her maids wrap her in muslin strips. She used sand and sugar to wash her face. It became an obsession."

"Did it keep her young?"

"No. No, Strawberry, that did not keep her young."

His tone didn't change but there was something, a faint twist to his full and ridiculously kissable lips, a subtle movement that expressed sorrow. I could almost see the young man he had been, madly in love and unable to do anything about it. *He's still a vampire. Still your kidnapper.* I didn't have to care about his story. I didn't have to care about him. I was trying my very best not to. But the least I could do was listen. I wanted to know more of the story, and he seemed to want to tell it.

"After France, her temperament also changed. I thought merely that she was still agonizing over her illness and her brush with death, but she was longing for something, or someone else. I wanted more than anything to save her. But she wanted something I could not give her."

He took a long breath and rubbed his elegant fingers across his forehead. "I learned later that she'd met Rene, a vampire, in France. She coaxed him into coming to London, and then she began to coax him into turning her. I had no idea. I thought … I thought she no longer loved me. I thought she had gotten bored with me and had simply taken on a new lover. Rene was wild and dashing. He was always turning up at the strangest hours and was always full of life latest at night while the rest of us were yawning in our cups. I thought it was no wonder she had turned her affections away from me." Owen paused, staring up at the stars.

"I thought it was over, and tried to move on. One night, I noticed Adelle and Rene, out late on the street. He was being violent with her, and I saw red. I followed them as they went into her townhouse, and I heard her screaming. I ... I was so naïve. I thought that was my chance, to save her as I'd always wished I could. I burst into the house, and when I saw Rene on top of her ... I killed him. I ran him through with my sword."

A hush fell again. The only sounds were the crickets in the grass, and the tinkling fall of the pool's waterfall. I was breathless, tingling with anticipation, eager to hear more, but it was obvious the telling of it was hard on him.

"She looked up and her face was ... she was deathly pale, and at first I thought I had struck her as well, that my sword had run them both through. Then I realized she was bleeding from a wound on her breast that had not been made by me, but rather by Rene's teeth."

I reached up and brushed my fingers over the closed wound beneath my collarbone where Owen had bitten me.

"He ... evaporated. I can't describe it any other way. He turned to dust in front of my eyes. I was horrified and repulsed. I knew ... I had heard the stories of vampires, but to see it, I thought I would go mad."

I scoffed softly. *I could relate to that.*

"I wanted to save her, to keep her from that fate,

but there was no going back for her, she had turned. She told me she needed blood or she would die. Rene had given her enough of his to turn her, but she had to feed. Part of me knew the best thing to do would be to kill her. Just run her through and allow her soul to be judged, but I couldn't do it."

His voice actually broke, and I saw a glint on his cheek that couldn't be anything except a tear. "I loved her too much. I could not kill the woman I loved."

A huge, salty lump rose in my throat. My chest felt tight, and my heart literally ached. I had never loved anyone that much, and it didn't seem like I would ever get the chance given my circumstances, but I wanted to. I wanted to love so much that impossible choices made sense.

I should have stopped the words that came from my mouth next, but in the usual fashion, they spilled anyway, making a mess. "But you did. You did kill her."

Owen's head swung around to glare at me. "Out of the water. It's time to go back to your room."

I stood, dumbstruck. I would have kicked myself if my foot wasn't already wedged in my mouth.

Owen reached down and grabbed me under my shoulders, hoisting me out of the pool and onto the pebbled edge in one swift motion. Water ran off me, pooling under my feet. Owen still gripped me, standing before me like a vengeful god.

unLife

I reached up to touch his face, a motion of comfort, of apology. He snatched my hand and squeezed it between us.

I stammered and shook my head. "I'm sorry. I was just more confused than anything, I mean, about why. Thank you for telling me your story, for opening up to me. I can't imagine what you've been through, what you've suffered. To still be this much of a man, a good man—kidnapping aside—is a miracle. I just wish I could understand you more, maybe heal anything in you that hurts." I didn't even know what I was saying, words spilled out of my mouth as my heart ached in unwanted sympathy for him.

So many emotions flashed through his expression. He seemed so human now. Not just from him revealing his past, but from the level of emotion and compassion and vulnerability I saw in those dark eyes.

His voice was a tortured whisper. "I did. I did kill her." His eyes closed, and he buried his face in my neck. I thought for a moment he would bite me, but instead, he just rested his face there, cool cheek against my skin. His fingers reached up and twisted into my hair. And he held me like that as time stood still around us.

The water dripping off me, and the cool air left me chilled. Owen's lifeless body did nothing to warm me. A succession of shivers shuddered through me, encouraged by my confused emotions.

"What if this is my curse, to kill the women I—" His body tensed around mine then he backed away. His face was a mixture of fury and confusion which left me shaking even harder.

His eyes landed on my almost naked body and softened. "You're cold."

I nodded, teeth chattering.

Silently, he lifted me up, my body limp and limbs heavy as he carried me upstairs to my bedroom.

I resisted kittenishly as he laid me down, hiding my wrist. But he did not try to cuff me. Instead, he laid down beside me, drawing me into the hollow under his arm.

He nuzzled into my neck, and his teeth sank gently into the skin. I relaxed, allowing it to happen. That slow languor that was left over from my swim drifted into something else, something so sweet and golden edged that I embraced it. The soft heat of blood flowing from me to him was such an intimate connection, a crimson thread connecting us.

His teeth left my flesh, but he remained curled around me. He whispered, "Thank you, for listening."

His cool body wrapped around me and I faded into sleep. In the hazy, dreamlike moments before slumber took me, he whispered again, so softly it felt like the wind from the distant mountains. "Strawberry. I don't know what to do with you."

unLife

I woke up several hours later.

Owen was still asleep beside me, and dawn peeked under the drawn curtains, a blaze of pink and gold. I blinked, feeling a bit disoriented, and then I moved my leg that had been tucked under Owen's.

The chain rattled. I stared at it in utter disbelief. He had chained me again, despite the fact he was in the bed next to me. Anger swelled under my skin, flaring red hot.

I didn't know what to think, what to do. I went and locked myself in the bathroom until I heard him leave, then returned to bed to sleep out the daylight. I blinked back tears that made no sense as I settled back under the covers that still smelled like him.

12

I awoke around midday. Lying in bed, staring at the ceiling, I played through what had happened last night, and what in all-mighty fuck it could have meant. Who cuddled up to and slept with their captor? This idiot. I had tried to remain detached, but Owen and his damn heartbreak edged in under my armor, and the thought of pushing him away after that had felt too hard.

I *liked* having him next to me, holding me tight. I grunted and kicked at the sheets. I did *not* care about him. I just needed to release the pent-up energy and angst brought on by the vampire opening up to me like some tragic Victorian romance hero. It probably didn't mean a god damned thing. Still, I didn't know where I stood anymore. Had our relationship changed?

When I finally sat up, the room, at least, had changed. I stared at the wide-open armoire, not quite sure that my mind wasn't playing tricks on me. Clothes overflowed from it, heaps of silk, satin, and lace in exquisite colors. My eyes couldn't turn away.

I got up and went to the wardrobe, my fingers stroking the garments lovingly. They all looked incredibly expensive—the perfect cut and exquisite fabrics gave that away. When I had first arrived in Hollywood, I had been wearing designer labels head-to-toe. The clothes I had worn then had names screaming from their back pockets, or across the chest. I wore them until a producer told me that wealthy people never wore such garish things. Very wealthy people wore clothes that were incredibly expensive due to the cost of the workmanship and materials, not the cost of the giant letters emblazoned on them. By wearing those clothes, I was marking myself as a rube.

I had learned to scour the thrift shops and consignment stores, looking not at names of designers on the outside of the clothes, but the things that most people never thought to look for. I had a small amount of incredibly good stuff that was pre-owned, which Lisa always seemed to get her mitts on, but I had never held anything brand new in my hands before.

Alongside the couture fashion were some equally quality comfy clothes; organic cotton singlets, yoga pants and merino hoodies. *How strange.*

There was a heavy white envelope on the dresser. I opened it and pulled out the elegant stationary within. A man's strong, back-slanting handwriting met my eyes, and I traced the letters with one finger, knowing it could only be Owen's.

These are for you. Over the years I have developed a taste for the luxuries in life. I can most certainly afford the finest of things, and I have been remiss in not providing you with clothing and other necessities. I ask your forgiveness for that oversight. Immortality has also taught me the value of comfort, so I hope you will find some comfort in this selection. The emerald green and gold dress is the one I would like to see you in at dinner. Please be ready at exactly eleven pm. This will be a formal dining occasion.

I read the words twice, and then found the gown he had referred to in his note. It was a marvelous confection of dark green silk that I knew would cling like a second skin. The top was a corset type thing, woven through with metallic gold thread. The laces tied tightly on the back, but closer inspection revealed a tiny and nearly invisible zipper on the right side that would make it easy for me to dress myself.

I went a little crazy pawing through the selection. There were not just outer garments but undergarments as well, lacy bra and panty sets, sheer stockings, and even shoes of all different heel types and styles.

I hugged a swimsuit to my body and danced around a bit wildly in a burst of exhilarated joy.

All the clothes were just my size and for an hour or so I delighted in trying them on, preening, and primping, caught up in the excitement of it all. I mostly tried on the dresses, which made up the bulk of the clothing. I wanted to put some new panties on since I'd been wearing my old ones for far, far too long, but had no idea how I was meant to do that with a chain around my ankle. It took me half an hour to work out I had to feed the fabric through the gap between the cuff and my skin. That was when reality crashed in.

I was still chained up. I had not won any freedom.

I hadn't succeeded in making Owen see me as human. I had simply succeeded in earning the status of a spoiled little pet, a comical little pooch, or ... I shuddered, remembering Loretta calling me Meow Kitty. I was no more cared for than one of those little dogs toted around in a specially designed purse. I was just a belonging to Owen, still a prisoner. A prisoner with comforts, but no less a possession.

My happiness deflated as though it were a leaky balloon. I crumpled onto the bed, head flopping over the side, and stared at the heaps of gorgeous things, feeling my humanity slipping away. What hurt the worst was that I *had* started to care about him, despite every effort not to, despite him being a vampire. It was the human-ness he had displayed lately that made me care about him. Yet he seemed determined to turn me into a mere object, a prettily dressed and plated meal, a pet who would eventually give her life for his.

The chain was a hateful but visible reminder of how little I should trust him. I was no better off than a cute Chihuahua that was dressed in a funny suit then tethered in the yard so it didn't run for the road.

The darkness inside me grew more complete and I had no energy left to reach for the light. Depression weighed me down so much that I literally sagged into the mattress. How did I put a screeching halt to this before I gave in entirely? Before I let my life be taken from me, one way or another?

With my head tilted back at that angle, a reflection of light behind the side table caught my eye. I looked again, my heart doing little jumping jacks when I realized what I saw.

Loretta's cleaver.

It lay hidden under the bedside table, only a thin wedge of its handle showing. She must have dropped it there before going feral and chasing me to her death. Owen had cleaned the room afterwards, but he must have missed it. It had been lying there, hidden from both of us for all this time.

I dropped to my knees and picked it up. It was real and solid in my hands. A giggle, born of hysteria,

bubbled out of my mouth.

I tested the edge with my thumb. *Ouch, sharp!*

I caught my breath at the enormity of the possibilities. I could hack my way through the chain or try to hack out the section of bedpost that the chain was attached to. If it came to it, could I cut my foot off to free my ankle? Or could I just kill Owen when he came to have dinner, stick the cleaver into his neck and cut his bloodsucking head right off his shoulders?

That last thought made me go cold. *Could I do that to him?* No. I didn't think I could. I wanted to hate him, to think of him as only a heartless monster, but the truth was some part of him was human. I had seen it with my own eyes. I could not kill that person.

I set to work on the bed, figuring I might need my foot at some point for a successful escape. Half an hour later, I stared at the barely splintered post in disbelief wondering if I really did need my foot. It would have been easier and likely less messy to simply chop it off. The post was solid as a rock, ugly gouges and deep scars marred it, but it still held.

I attacked it again, grunting and trembling with exertion. There was a strange groan and hunk of wood fell away. It was taking too long. I could sense the hours slipping away. I could almost feel the night, and Owen, approaching. I hit the post with the cleaver again with renewed vigor, only to have the cleaver fall apart in my hands. The blade fell to the mattress and I stared at the useless handle, wondering if this were all some cosmic joke.

The sky was warming outside, turning from blue to syrupy orange, dipping into night.

I tossed the handle and blade to the floor, then lay on my back. With a battle cry of frustration, I used both feet like a battering ram, kicking, even though it sent waves of pain through my legs. The post cracked, creaked, and then it toppled down, almost braining me in the process.

I sat up, tugging the chain at my ankle. It swung free against the bed and I shouted out, "Yes!"

The cuff was still locked firmly around my ankle, and the long length of chain attached to it, so I had to scoop it up and carry it. I was still wearing a shirt from my earlier dress ups, but no pants. There was no time for pants. Daylight had almost gone.

I didn't stop for anything. I ran down the stairs, pelting for the front door. I could see it right in front of me and I reached it, opened it, and almost cried at the sight of the front lawn, turned golden by the strong final rays of sunlight.

I had one foot out the door when an arm snaked around my middle and yanked me off my feet. All the air whooshed out of my diaphragm and I fought, flailing and kicking, beating at the hands that were tangled around my torso.

A soft, hissing sizzle filled my ears, and I choked on the smoky fumes clouding my eyes.

Owen cursed, but still held tight.

He dragged me back into the house.

"Let me go. Please, just let me go!" I howled and kicked at his shins.

Owen turned me around to face him. His skin showed signs of ash and burns, but healed before my eyes.

I had been so close. With freedom so near within reach, every fiber of me yearned for it. But at the same time, I felt at home within his arms. Confused, appalled, and at home. A rough sob tore out of my throat, and I wept loudly.

He dropped his forehead onto mine, still holding me tight, arms wrapped fully around me. "You can't leave, Strawberry. You can't leave me. Please don't leave me."

13

He held me until I ran out of tears. Then led me back to my room, and re-attached my chain to a different bedpost.

"Dress, and we will dine." His voice was commanding, but gentle.

I had nothing else left to do but obey. I moved like the living dead, all spirit and fight gone.

I discovered that the bathroom also had some new additions. High end organic hair products, and a few pieces of jewelry that matched the green dress he had asked me to wear. I found a clever little makeup kit, expensive as all hell and brand new. I would have killed to have it in my former life. Now, I just stared at it, empty and uncaring.

I showered, taking my time. I felt no need to

rush. I wasn't going anywhere. Owen wasn't going anywhere. I was stuck in this house with him forever and couldn't even bring myself to hate that outcome anymore. I'd all but given up.

I dried my hair and pulled it up. Looking in the mirror, I saw a vague and indefinable difference in my face. I was thinner, yes, but there was something else there too, something I could not put a finger on. Something like defeat.

I dipped the make-up brushes into the little pots of pure mineral pigment, smudging shadows around my eyes, and coloring in my lips. I plumped out my eyelashes and daubed blush on the apples of my cheeks.

I took the green dress off the hanger and shimmied it on over my head. The green and gold silk clung to my body like wet cloth, and the corset pressed my breasts into a perfect shape, rounding out the tops and accentuating the small puncture marks in them.

I put on the matching emerald earrings. *Those aren't real emeralds, are they?* But I couldn't bring myself to put the bracelet on. I couldn't have something around my wrist again.

I stepped out of the bathroom and found Owen waiting patiently in the middle of the bedroom.

My ire and sadness evaporated like mist before the sun. He looked splendidly handsome in an ebony suit with a scarlet silk shirt below it. His thin, black tie was perfect, his shoes shined to nearly nuclear glow, and his dark hair swept up and back from his forehead, accentuating the high angular planes of his face.

"You look beautiful," he said.

"You too." My voice sounded weak and thin. My heart fluttered like a schoolgirl's, and I could not stop looking at his broad shoulders, the way his fingers lightly rested against his thighs, and the long sweep of his lean legs. There was a little color in his cheeks, just a hint of rosiness high on the cheekbones, and his eyes were paler than I'd ever seen them.

"I like your hair up."

I touched it self-consciously. I was way overdue for a trim and I had not had access to a straightener in … *How long had I been here?* My hair had returned to its naturally wavy state, and even though I had pinned it up, small curls escaped to frame my face. I had outlined my eyes dramatically, using long sweeps of eyeliner and a rich gold-green shadow, as well as a lot of mascara. His eyes said he approved of me entirely and I felt a flush of pleasure at his obvious desire.

Here he stood, the monster who'd robbed me of my freedom, who'd caught me and crushed my hopes of escape just moments before, and we were playing out some dress up fantasy like kids on prom night. I felt

strangely hollow, like all my emotions were happening on my skin but not actually reaching inside me. I think he noticed because his smile faltered.

He walked up to me and scooped me into his arms. "Trust me."

I nodded, absently. I did trust him, in a way. He held my life in his hands every day since he'd stolen my freedom. I knew he would protect my life, if nothing else.

He moved so fast, all I sensed was a rush of speed and blurring landscape.

One minute we were in the house, the next, we were standing on a mountain top. A few tall trees created a wall on one side, and the scent of pine hovered thickly in the air, mixing with the smell of ocean drifting from a cliff down the rocky slope.

"Where are we?" My eyes darted left and right, hoping to see a house, or a car, or any sign of civilization, but it was just us high on a windswept peak.

"Come, sit."

A table stood to the right, draped in fine white linens, laid with china so thin it was nearly transparent, and a selection of wine bottles formed a centerpiece. French champagne, a rich, deep red, and a bottle of German ice wine, accompanied by appropriate glassware for each. Silver domed trays covered the table, and I walked to it, numbed and uncertain. Was this real?

unLife

Had he put me under a spell? The last time he'd tried, it didn't work. But I was still confused. He had no maid anymore that I knew of.

"Are the catering staff hiding behind the trees? Or ..."

He grinned, a boyish and charming quirk of his lips that melted my heart. "I did this for you. I have always cooked for you, Strawberry."

Oh, that figured. Gorgeous, rich, and a good cook. Of course, he was a bloodsucking kidnapper and killer; he had to have some kind of fucking fault.

His hand was cold on my back as he pulled out my chair and seated me. How ironic that a vampire had better manners than most guys I had dated. I gratefully accepted a glass of sparkling champagne, the fizz bringing notes of apple and oak into my nose.

Owen extended an empty glass to mine, chinking gently, before serving my dinner.

"What's the occasion?" I asked. Don't get me wrong, I didn't want to look a gift vampire in the mouth, but I wasn't used to being spoiled like this. Ever. Even with human men.

Owen paused with my plate in his hand. I wished I hadn't asked the question at that moment because I wanted that food. Now.

He smiled softly and replied, "You provide me with delicious sustenance. I simply felt the urge to return the favor."

"I would say aaaw, but it's not a favor really, now is it, if I have no choice in the matter?" I snapped at him, but was smiling as well. A mischievous mood had taken over. *Holy hot dogs. Am I flirting with him?*

The thought was wiped away by the appearance of sea scallops ceviche. The dish was bursting with the flavors of the citrus marinade that cooked the scallops, leaving them tender and supple. Maybe it was the food, but I felt my hollowness beginning to subside, drowned out by an eagerness for fine dining, good company, and my own desire to be normal, or at least pretend for a little while.

The bread he sliced and put on my side plate was crusty outside, fluffy and filled with air pockets inside. The butter melted into it and I sopped up marinade with the tail end of the bread, not caring about my manners.

Owen watched me curiously.

I spoke through a half-full mouth. "I bet your fancy old-fashioned girls ate all pretty like."

"They did. They even took classes to teach them to eat properly."

"What did they even eat back then? Potatoes? Gruel? Put a plate like this in front of anyone and I dare them not to lick it clean."

Owen laughed. "I do enjoy seeing the pleasure you take in your meals."

Ditto. The thought hit me with shock, remembering

a time when Owen sunk his teeth into my thigh. I fanned my heated cheeks and shook the thought away.

Next up was a salad with grilled peaches and goat cheese as the main flavor points. I was on the verge of proposing long before the duck confit showed up. I was beyond sated. Owen had poured the wine generously into my glass throughout the meal, and I was tipsy from alcohol and the surfeit of food.

Placing the last bite of juicy duck into my mouth, I let out a long, low moan that sounded truly sexual. Good food really did turn me on.

"Enjoying yourself?" Owen asked, an eyebrow raised.

"Uh huh," I murmured, leaning back in the chair, basking in the fullness of my stomach. "Some entertainment would have been nice with the dinner though. You could hula dance naked on the table for me."

I thought dinner was done, but with a truly wicked smile, Owen retrieved the final dish. He bent on one knee and opened the dome in front of me, like opening a diamond ring box. I squeed and said, "Yes, yes, yes!"

The chocolate soufflé was light, high, and so beautiful it seemed almost a sin to break its surface. Not that I minded being a sinner. I certainly wasn't going to let its looks, or the fact that my belly was protruding horribly, stop me.

I raised a bite of it to my mouth and he said, "Tell me how it tastes."

I tried to, but I wasn't sure he understood. How many years had it been since he'd had real food? I felt pity for him again, not being able to enjoy things like chocolate and wine must truly suck. I felt myself stumbling over my words the same way I had the other night at the pool, and I blushed at my own incompetence. He didn't seem to mind though. He just watched me, his eyes full of a shimmering, vulnerability that seemed far too human.

14

The meal ended and my belly felt swollen and too full, but it was a good feeling. The wind had picked up. It rustled through the trees and sent tiny leaves shivering down onto my shoulders. Under my bare feet the earth was still warm from the day. My toes dug into a loamy layer of dead leaves and pine needles gone soft from rain and wind. The small tendrils of my hair that had escaped the knot I had pulled it up into, lifted from my face and neck. The sky was ebony, a few clouds scuttled across its surface, and the bright stars pricked the sooty colored down with gleaming sparkles of light. It was so exquisite that a lump rose into my throat.

Owen helped me up from the table and we wandered down to the edge of the cliff. I gazed at the jumble of boulders and the shimmering motion of the tide far below. A ledge sat about halfway down the mountainside, a glittering streak of mica running through it. Dread coiled into my belly. What if I fell? My toes curled into the edge and I heard tiny pebbles rattling and sliding down the sides of the mountain.

Owen wrapped his strong arms around me. The intense cold coming from his body made me shiver as I leaned against him. I rested my head on his chest, hoping to hear a heartbeat, but there was nothing, just the feel of his body beneath mine.

"Trust me, Strawberry," he said.

Then he jumped.

We went over, and that time I didn't scream. I had learned to trust him, to know he wouldn't let me fall. That trust made me immensely sad. The first guy in my entire life that I trusted was not only going to hurt me but eventually kill me. I tried to ignore the tightness in my chest, forcing myself to take a breath, and hoped my shudders would be mistaken for nerves rather than sorrow.

Owen floated easily to the ground with me still clasped in his arms. The tang of the sea was tangible. The sound of the waves slapping the shore, and an occasional caw from a nocturnal bird, fired up my emotions. The ragged remains of the depression lifted, and I laughed loudly as we landed in the sand.

unLife

The mountain loomed over us and the lights of a jet plane winked red overhead. I could hear a faint music—a sign of life existing far beyond the confines of the world that only included Owen and me.

Owen carried me easily. My arms were still wound around his neck and his scent came to me, a little musky and coppery. The smell of blood and cologne.

He let me down and we stood together, watching the waves nip at our toes. A swell ran across my bare feet, awash with shells and sand. As the salt water rushed over my skin, it stung the light abrasions left on my ankle from the cuff. Again, I was reminded that I was nothing more than a pet on a very long leash. Hatred flared inside me. Even now, I wore the evidence of my imprisonment.

I stepped away from Owen, folding my arms against the sea breeze which suddenly left me chilled. I knew that the look I wore wasn't kind or happy. I could have been a queen in exile. Really, I was just a woman with nowhere to go, too stubborn to give in.

Owen asked, "If you could do one thing right now, anything, what would it be?"

"Escape." The word came to my lips instantly. I didn't even need to think. It was the truest answer I could give. No matter how attractive he was, how beautiful the clothes were, or how amazing the dinner, I was always going to try to escape. I wanted to agree to go to dinner, not be forced. I wanted to

buy my own clothes. I wanted to be free.

"That isn't possible for you."

"It is if you turn your back and let me run like heck," I said. I faced him, stalking him down. Every step forward I took, he took one back. "I'm never going to stop trying to get away. Until the day you kill me, I am going to want out. I will never be happy being a vampire's prisoner."

He stopped suddenly, before I could halt myself. I started backwards but tripped on the hem of the dress. One of his strong arms caught me around the waist as I dipped back, like the whole thing was choreographed. Our lips came close, so close I could feel a puff of cold air leave his and land on mine.

He brought me slowly up to my feet. His gaze was turned down, and brows lowered. "I see."

He lifted me into his arms but didn't speed us through the air in a flash. He walked at a regular, human pace along the beach. Cradled against his chest, the sound of the waves, the steady rock of his footsteps, and the heavy food and wine filling my belly, lulled me.

I awoke in a comfortable position, semi-reclined on a leather couch. It wasn't my room. Was it Owen's? The furniture was similar, but there was no window, and the bed had black sheets, shimmering like dark water under the low light. I didn't need to check to know I was chained to the bed. Owen sat at the other end of the lounge, holding a full glass of red wine, staring at it as though it was about to reveal the secrets of life itself.

"You're drinking wine?" I asked, skeptical of the scene before me.

"No. It turns to ash on my tongue. I don't know why I even tried, why I thought it would be different ..."

He set the glass down on the table beside him.

When he turned to me, his eyes were glossy, as though they were close to tears. He held me in his gaze.

"I've said how I feel you are changing me, how I didn't know whether I liked it. I know now. I do like it. I want this. But it torments me, as though something miraculous lies just out of reach. It torments me, because I feel the wrongs I have done you, but I cannot let you go."

He lifted a hand and stroked his fingers down my cheek, so softly I barely felt it. The touch made sparks leap between us—sparks neither of us could deny though we both knew we should. The moment hung suspended, rife with possibilities. I wanted him, and I could see it on his face—he wanted me, too.

Words shook from my lips. "You have changed. You seem so different to the vampire who first locked me up. He was cold, distant. Not anymore."

There was no accusation in his voice, only pain. "And yet you only want to flee from me."

Heat stung in my nose, and tears threatened.

I couldn't deny it any longer. I couldn't fight it. "I want my freedom. But I don't want to flee from you."

I had never seen him so open, so warm. His hand cupped my jaw and he leaned close, touching his forehead to mine.

"Kitty," he whispered.

I almost sobbed. "Owen."

Our lips met in a kiss that left me shaken to the cells of my being. He always elicited a primal response in me, one that was as thrilling as it was frightening. Sensations broke out along my nerve endings and my skin raised with gooseflesh. My tongue met his and tangled, slid away, met again. Passion left me dizzy.

His fingers brushed across my skin, tracing lines of desire over my bare shoulders and arms. I slowly worked to free his tie, slide back his jacket. I took time to caress each button of his shirt as I pushed it open, revealing his chest inch by inch.

Owen tugged at the lace up binding of my corset. I was about to reach for the hidden zipper when he took the strong layered fabric in two hands and tore it off me. I threw myself back into his arms, pressing my bare chest against his. When I licked along his neck and sucked at his earlobe, he groaned deeply, pulling me into his lap and running a hand under the silk skirt, up my legs. My mouth opened in a silent, helpless plea of longing.

UnLife

Desire built through my body to an almost unbearable ache. He pushed me back, flat onto the lounge, hands running across my chest, belly, hips, gently torturing me with his cold touch on my skin. He kissed his way down between my breasts, looped his tongue around my navel, then kissed the soft skin of my inner thigh. My eyes rolled with pleasure and I wanted nothing more than Owen, Owen, Owen.

He stood up, taking me with him, and placed me on the bed, laying me down so carefully. I felt fragile and cherished all at once. It was a giddy moment, made more so by the rush of lustful longing when he whipped off his belt and let his pants fall away.

He moved over me, bringing his weight down carefully, his dark eyes seeking mine for consent, for assurance. I nodded, wrapping my hands into his hair and kissing him deeply.

We cried out together as we joined. Pleasure shattered all of my defenses. I had no reservation, no hesitation. All I knew was the incredibly powerful need that built up inside me at his every touch and caress.

I kissed his neck, right in the hollow where his shoulder and collarbone met, and slid my hands up his back, relishing his weight and the reality of him. Our bodies rocked together in a slow, gentle, intense rhythm, and I whispered, "Take my blood, Owen. It's yours."

I had never before surrendered to his teeth, not truly. I had merely tolerated the bite, as a means to an end. Now, I offered my blood, my life, willingly. I was his.

His teeth slid into my skin. He drank and kissed and sucked at my neck. My eyes closed, and I gasped. A sweet ache spread from my toes to my scalp. A powerful need was obvious in his touch as he pushed into me, filling me, drinking my blood deeply, his arms wrapping me so tight I thought I would break. Something was happening. His body was growing warmer than it ever had before.

That shift from cold to hot within me knocked me senseless, and my body shuddered and locked tightly as pleasure hit me like a wall. Owen also cried out, clutching wildly at his chest in a gesture that scared me witless. A gesture full of pain, and terror, and disbelief.

He stumbled off me, backing away across the room. His fingers were interlocked over his heart, and his eyes had gone a strange shade of ... blue?

I stared at those eyes, at the terrified expression on his face, speechless and confused. He fled, literally fled from me, and I could only stare in total bewilderment as he streaked across the room and out the door.

"Maybe there was too much garlic in my blood, and he got heartburn?"

The joke fell flat, a desperate and failed attempt

to keep myself from falling into despair. My voice quavered, and tears slid down my face. I felt naked and exposed, not only because I actually was but because shame and confusion had set in.

Daylight splashed in through the open door, and from somewhere in the house there was a wounded howl. My skin prickled, and I crawled under the covers, smashing myself flat and as small as possible. Fear broke out along my spine. I shivered, while the rich food roiled and tumbled in my belly.

I lay there, looking up at the ceiling for what seemed like an eternity, waiting for him to come in and kill me for seducing him. Or to find out my blood had killed him, and I would die here alone, chained in this room. Or that he'd decided he didn't like the way I was changing him, and it was time to finish this. I waited for the end of the world I knew.

It didn't come.

The tension drew out nearly unbearably, but eventually my mind and body could take no more, and I drifted off into a dream-filled and restless sleep, marked by nightmares of Owen burning in the sunlight.

15

Sometime in the afternoon, I crawled out from under the covers, threw on Owen's shirt that had been left in a crumple beside the bed, and began to prowl around the room. The shirt still smelled like him. I clutched the silk tight around me, rolling my shoulders in it to feel it slip against my skin, shocked at my body's immediate, visceral reaction to the smell that I associated so closely with the man. The vampire. The man. The vampire.

The chain yanked me up short every time I reached its boundaries, and I screamed in anger and misery. The screams ripped from my throat and chest, leaving a pain in my body but clearing my mind.

The room had few to no personal effects. Just clothing, some cologne in the bathroom, and several ancient books stacked on the bedside table. But the ghost of his presence burned me. I kicked the wall and tossed a lampstand over, shattering the stained-glass shade. I felt like a rock star trashing a fancy hotel room. Everything just piled up and I couldn't help it, I needed to destroy. The wine glass and bottle on the coffee table were the first victims, shattering on the wall and staining the thick carpet. I pulled the bookcases down and flipped the couch over.

It was when I tossed the bedside table to one side that one of the books popped open, catching my eye. The book had a fake interior, and a small purse tumbled out. I got on my knees and looked at it. It was a lovely little thing, with silver clasps and gold embroidery. The name stitched into it made me catch my breath. *Adelle St Delaurents.*

I opened the purse with trembling fingers to see a diary, bound in leather and marked in place by a silk ribbon that was a mottled, faded gray. It was so small, it must have been made to be carried in a tiny bag, or in a small pocket. A lady's pocket.

I opened the diary and began to read.

Adelle's handwriting was rounded and flowing. It was also tiny, and when I closed her journal, my head ached fiercely from the strain of it all.

Owen had been right about her. Adelle had loved an adventure. She had seen him as one as well, a young and handsome man she could kiss and flirt with, ride at full gallop next to, dance wildly until dawn with, but long before he had ever seen her, she had been betrothed to her husband. A husband she never had any intention of ditching. But Owen had been exciting, and the fact that he fell in love with her just made her giddy. It made her feel important to have him lusting after her. It gave her an incredible feeling of power, that she could manipulate him so blindly.

Where Owen had gotten it wrong was in assuming she wanted him just as badly. Adelle wrote of her manipulations and flirtations, always finding them amusing. Like the other men she kept on her string, Owen was nothing more than a flirtation, a way of passing the time and ensuring her dance card was always full at the countless balls and parties she attended. She never let any of her beaus go any further than kisses and groping up her legs, because she was shrewdly and acutely aware that to do so would be to ruin her prospects for marriage.

When she did wed, and realized she no longer had to stay a virgin to ensure her place in society, she began to take on numerous lovers, of which Owen was just one.

He had no idea. She dangled her love in front of him for her own amusement. Her husband was indeed a cruel man, who treated her with little more than contempt or rage at her inability to produce a child, but she was cruel as well. More than cruel,

really. She seemed to accept her husband's treatment as normal, not going to any great lengths to avoid the punishments. Indeed, with delight she wrote about the color of the bruises that blossomed on her skin, and how the marks enraged Owen and the other lovers she kept on with lies of love and faithfulness. How she so enjoyed seeing the fury and passion it provoked in them, she made sure she always had some mark upon her skin.

When she was whisked away to France, she became infatuated with Rene, a handsome man with *'ebony hair and eyes, a walk that makes me shiver as it speaks of danger with every step, and an endless hunger for life nothing seems to assuage.*

'From the moment we met I could feel a need for him, a starving and thirsting need that would not, has never, let me rest. I adore him, despite his odd ways and violence in lovemaking. Just a fortnight ago he kissed my bosom so fiercely that he left a bite there, which made me so weak I could scarcely stand for days. The weakness passed but the bite remained in full view, making it necessary for me to stay in bed for days playing at megrims and other illness in order to keep anyone from seeing it, especially my hardly beloved husband. He would kill me if he knew I was once again cuckolding him, but I think Rene would be worth dying for.

'He manages to come into the house at all hours

of the night, unseen by the servants or passersby on the street. He always smells of wind and places that I have never been. Oh! To be with him there and forever!'

If Rene were anything like Owen, I could understand the attraction. But not wholly. When Owen was a vampire, that turned me off completely. What made me care about him was his human behavior: his kindness and vulnerability. It was when he was at his most unvampire-like best that I ...

Oh shit ...

I blocked that thought before it could work its way into my head. I could not possibly be in love with him. It just wasn't possible. Not even if he was great in bed and a damn good cook. No way.

I turned my attention back to Adelle. Rene had bitten her, and she had gone into a serious depression when she was hauled back to merry old England. Bored and lonely, she had turned to Owen, feeding him tales of her love for him. She claimed that she had been unable to see him, abed with excuses of ill-health, and that she had gone to France to see a doctor. All these lies and stories she'd concocted, I don't know how she kept up with them. If anything, Adelle sounded like a more accomplished actress than I was.

There was a sharp shift in her writing around then as well. It was as though Rene's bite had made her somehow terribly aware of her own mortality. Was it possible she had known that he was a vampire? I believed she had, and she longed to be young and beautiful forever as well, to be able to keep her lovers enchanted and on her strings.

When Rene came after her, she was ready for him, seducing him and using him just as she did all men. Together they had turned her husband into a thrall. He was seen in public and acted as normal as could be managed. He rode in carriages and attended balls for short amounts of time before pleading illness and leaving. Rene and Adelle kept him prisoner for nearly two months before she managed to convince Rene to bite her. I think she had some idea that the two of them would float through high society, with wealth and power, together. I think she may have really loved him, despite how she tried to use him. Though I didn't know much about Rene, what she said of him made me wonder if he was playing her as much as she was playing him.

That was when things got very out-of-control. Owen came upon them together. Everything he had told me about the night he had been turned had been true, with one exception. Adelle had been a vampire for weeks. She had simply lied so he would not kill her too. She promised him that her love was still true, and drank from him as greedily as if he were a giant-sized cherry Slurpee.

But Owen had bitten her back. He had known,

somewhere deep down, that she was a liar, that she meant to simply drain him and dispose of him. He had bitten her wrist in a frenzied moment, and she had been too caught up in feeding from him to stop him until it was too late. Adelle had been amused by his biting her, by the sudden and startling rebellion against her pretty lies. She had also thought it sexy as hell.

So, she kept him around. While Owen was busy searching for a cure for them, Adelle began to hunt, not just for food, but also for sport and to increase her wealth. Owen drank but never killed. Adelle saw that as a weakness. She thought it was just because he was still new, and that as his humanity was left further behind, he would become like her. She always killed her prey, often haunting the places where men with money went, so she would have cash on hand to support her ever-increasing love for luxuries. They had argued about it more than once. It was clear she began to tire of the rules and boundaries he tried to lay, and his attachment to being human. In some of their darker moments as a couple, they discovered the law that vampires could not kill other vampires, not without receiving an even worse punishment from others of their kind.

Over time, Owen drifted away from Adelle, and started to build businesses on his own labors and small inheritance. He began running a tavern, only

open at nighttime, so it would seem natural he only appeared then to manage the business.

Dark Raine. Duh. I mentally face-palmed. He must own the club the LARP was at. More than that, I was sure it was a worldwide chain.

Owen annoyed Adelle with his constant need to be returned to his human state, and his ongoing love for her only made her angry. She viewed him as a weight, and since her husband had died while still in thrall, she set out to find a lover that would be willing to kill Owen.

I could have killed Adelle for that. She bewitched a wealthy man, then told him that Owen was a vampire. He raised a mob and they came after Owen. Owen managed to escape and, in fury, Adelle killed her latest lover for failing.

The diary ended there; the next few pages torn out.

I threw it at the wall in frustration.

16

"I see you are reading."

Owen appeared behind me. I spun around and my mouth dropped open. His face was positively glowing with warmth, and his eyes were still that same light shade of blue. He was wearing jeans, something I had never seen him wearing, and a plain white shirt.

A very different presence radiated from him, but I couldn't put my finger on what it was. Some emotion on his face, hard, but human, relieved, but desperately sad. Still, he didn't seem pissed at finding me digging around in his dead lover's belongings, so I answered honestly. "Yes, I was."

He bent down and retrieved the diary from where it had fallen. He stared at it for a long time. "I suppose you think me a fool."

I huffed. "I've done some crazy shit because of love, too."

A smile turned the corners of his full lips upward. "Really?"

I deflected, playing down any meaning to my words. "Who hasn't?"

He leaned over and his shirt pulled up to reveal the smooth flesh above his waistband. Owen slipped the diary into the purse and then back into the fake book.

"I am guessing you want to know what happened."

"She tried to have you killed, then it just ends."

"Would you believe I had loved her for more than a hundred years at that point, and was still blind to her nature? She was cruel and corrupted, but when I looked at her all I saw was beauty. All I saw was the one I loved, once, when I was human. I held onto my love for her as I held onto my humanity, or at least, the pretense of humanity. I hadn't been human for a long time at that point. I had forgotten how to truly feel anything. I couldn't love, couldn't show compassion or empathy. I had set myself rules and morals which I stuck to, but not for any form of kindness. Only to be clever, for self-preservation. And she did not agree with those rules. When I confronted her, she laughed at me and said she had never loved me, that she would never love me, and

UnLife

that I was weak."

He closed his eyes, lost in the memory, and I found myself longing for them to open again, so I could stare at that new shade of blue.

"I wanted to be horrified by her actions, but I could feel nothing. I left, going to my offices to get some peace and to think. All the blood, all of those years, my mortal life, wasted. All of the killing she had done, all the people no longer on the earth for no purpose but to serve her selfish need to be beautiful, to be wealthy, and powerful, and worshipped. And yet, I couldn't feel. The smallest hint of sadness came to me for all I had lost, and then it too was gone. Only clear, emotionless decision remained."

I took a step closer to him, as though drawn in. He opened his eyes again, stepping back.

"A mob showed up with stakes and torches, they swarmed through the tavern and into my office, killing two of my human bartenders—good men making a living for their families. The mob dragged me out into the street and beat me, stabbed me with their stakes. They narrowly missed my heart and I had just enough strength left to flee. I staggered away, bloodied and dying. The first human to cross my path was a child. *A child.* I almost killed her trying to regain some strength and then, *then*, I didn't even care. I've committed too many inexcusable acts in my time."

I reached out a hand to Owen's, but he pulled away before I could touch him.

"I grew even colder and harder inside. I travelled abroad, seeking answers. I discovered that while vampires cannot kill one another directly, there is an ancient death curse for those who are corrupt. It was held within a silver ring that was possessed by the spirit of a vengeful ghost; a young woman killed wrongly."

Owen's gaze roamed around the room, anywhere but to me. His mouth grew tight. "I found the ring. The old Romani man who held it told me he could not give it to me, that the ring found those who deserved it. I told him of Adelle, and he said if she deserved punishment it would come.

"I went back to see Adelle. I had no plan, other than to try to make her see what she did was wrong, hoping time had changed her. Even if we as vampires couldn't feel, we could still decide how to behave based on the world around us. We didn't have to be monsters. When I opened her door, she was lying there on a chaise, her hand in the air and the ring on her finger. It could be no other, with an immense ruby cut like a drop of blood, the silver setting tarnished to black. She was admiring it, and I wanted to tell her to take it off, to save herself, but it was not up to me. That ring chooses its wearer.

"I said what I wanted to, then turned away. She

laughed at me but then she stopped. I did not turn around to see her die. I didn't need to. Her ashes drifted across the room in a stinking cloud. I dispersed her wealth to the poorest of the area, and left England for a new ... *life*."

"I'm so sorry." My heart ached for him, but he brushed my words aside.

"It's over now. I promise you, if I had not found your blood so sweet, so bewitching, I would never have held you prisoner. That has never been my way. I had my rules. Harvey sends porn actors to many a game at my club, and I've often taken them to feed from after the night has ended. But I have never killed any of them, never showed unneeded cruelty, nor kept them prisoner before, until you."

I choked. "I'm sorry, did you just imply I'm a porn actor?"

"What?" He blinked, looking clearly confused by my objection.

"Oh god, you think I'm a porn actress." I stared up at him.

His blue eyes bored into mine. "You're not a porn actress?"

"I'm not a porn actress!"

He put his hands over his face and laughed, huge gusty laughter.

"But you're so ..." He bit his bottom lip, looking over my body. "I just mean ..."

I considered the way I've acted under his captivity. I almost couldn't blame him for thinking that way. "I'm not, I'm really not. I am an actress, but I have never done porn. I'm the girl that always dies in the horror flicks before the hot blondes even start getting naked. It's sort of the formula, you know, geeky dark-haired girl with small tits gets chain sawed first, while the blonde with the giant bolt-on tits survives until the shower scene."

He looked completely nonplussed. "Bolt-on tits?"

Leave it to a guy to focus on that.

He shook his head. "I'm sorry I assumed you were. Kitty French sounds somewhat like a porn star's name."

Ouch. I glared at him. "Not hardly. I mean … okay, it might, maybe, a little …" It did. *Shit.* I had taken to using Kitty instead of Kaitlyn when I first moved to Hollywood, to be a new me, and all I did was make myself sound like a porn star. "That does not mean I am though."

"He said you were."

"Who?" Even as I asked, I knew the answer. *Harvey! That bastard.* He had sent me on a porn job after all. I wondered if he knew the real fate he was sending those girls to? A bit of role playing, and a quick bite from a real-life vampire. Owen must have had his pick of hot bodies to drink from. My stomach gurgled with jealousy.

"You didn't, you know, sleep with all the porn actresses as well as bite them, did you?"

Owen glanced at his feet, a gorgeous, bashful motion that made my heart backflip. "No, you're the only one."

We stared at each other, and I couldn't get over the shade of blue his eyes had turned. Like ashen cornflowers, or a dusky winter sky. His face grew solemn, and in that frown, tiny lines of age showed around his eyelids.

"Your eyes, they're … You've changed." I reached up toward his face, but he took a step back before I could touch him.

"Can you ever forgive me, Strawberry?" There was something strange about his voice, so sorrowful. I didn't understand, but it made my soul ache.

"Forgive you for what? I'm sure girls are confused for porn stars all the time. I mean, there was the whole kidnapping thing …" I tried to make it sound light, but I could see a darkness closing over Owen.

The dim light from the hallway stroked the planes of his face while he paused for a moment, then said, "I am so sorry, Strawberry. Maybe one day you will find it in your heart to forgive me, but I don't know how you ever could. You shouldn't. Not for what I've done to you."

Owen left me there and didn't come back, though I waited for hours. I lay on my back, staring at the

shifting shadows on the ceiling, and alternating between wanting to scream, cry, and laugh hysterically. It's a good thing I couldn't get to the kitchen since I was ripe for a peanut butter jar and a spoon kind of moment. I missed ice cream. I really, really did. To keep myself amused, or maybe just to add a little salt to the wound, I thought of gelato, Italian ices, and waffle cones. Rainbow sprinkles and hot fudge poured liberally over soft serve. I dreamed about mint chocolate chip, and the delicious texture of cookie dough ice cream. Eventually, daydreaming turned into real dreaming. I welcomed the escape of sleep gratefully.

17

I woke up in my own bedroom with the sun shining through the open balcony doors. Funny how I'd come to think of it as mine when I was just being kept prisoner there. It was like possession made it better somehow. I rolled over on my side, prepared to face another day in captivity. My feet hit the floor and I pushed myself up so I could head to the bathroom. Apart from a few birds chirping, the house was strangely silent.

I was halfway there when I realized what the silence meant. I had grown so used to the clatter and chatter of the chain that I no longer heard it, until I didn't. I looked down and stared at my ankle. It was red and chafed, the skin abraded in places, but it was free of the cuff. I shook my head and pinched myself. Surely, I was dreaming still.

But I wasn't. I glanced at my wrist. It still showed some abrasion marks from the cuff, though it was mostly healed. On my other wrist, marks from Owen's fangs were only small, red dots.

Confusion set in, and I felt fear creep over my thoughts. What if this was all some sick game, like where the predator pretended to let a prisoner go just so they could capture them again for the thrill of it? I really did think in movie terms, but it came with the job.

There was a neatly folded slip of paper on the dresser. My hands shook when I opened it. The words made my stomach clench into knots.

You are free of me, Strawberry. Go. Do not try to come back or find me, I will not be here, and I do not want to see you again. Enjoy your life, Kitty, may it be better than you imagined it could be.

I read over the note three times, carefully taking in the words.

I was pissed as hell. How cowardly of him to break up with me in a note! Wait, did I just think that? This wasn't a breakup. It was the release of a prisoner. I should be grateful, and I was. I'd gotten what I'd been fighting for. I longed to be outside of the walls of this house of horrors, but another part of me was saddened by the prospect, and more than a little scared. My feelings about Owen were still so conflicted, a mingle of desperation, fear, love, and anger.

Below the note was a small black bag. I opened it and a stack of hundred-dollar bills greeted me. Hello! I had a vivid image of myself throwing it on the bed and rolling around, but it quickly faded. I counted one stack then estimated the rest—there had to be at least ten grand there. What was this? Some kind of victims' compensation?

I needed to leave, but I just stood there feeling incredibly uncertain. As weird as it was, that was the first time I didn't want to run away. Last night had been amazing. Owen's humanity had shone through, past any monster in him, and the sight had been incredible to behold. I wanted to talk to him, learn more from him. I wanted to touch him, and comfort him when he got that lost look in his eyes. Those new, incredible blue eyes.

I was free, but I could not leave. There was a pile of new clothes on the dresser, too—jeans in my size, a pretty top I would have bought myself, and a bra and panty set decorated with strawberries. The set was almost childish, but it made tears burst from my eyes. He had left, but I was still his Strawberry.

Stockholm syndrome much? The nasty little voice in my head startled me and I spun around, looking to see if there was anyone else in the room. That voice sounded nothing like the voice I used to talk to myself. It sounded older, cynical and tired. My shoulders

slumped. I was all of those things, and heartbroken to boot. I felt much older. Or maybe just wiser.

I got dressed, brushed my teeth and hair, and stared at my face in the mirror. My first neck wound was healing, but would leave a scar. On the other side, two tiny red marks from last night showed. My skin had regained a bit of color but not enough. I was eerily pale. Under my eyes there were slight lavender-colored circles, and my cheekbones had hollowed. I still had bruises on my arms and shoulders from hitting the wall while escaping from Loretta. There were also the marks of the cuff, but otherwise I looked … damn good. Like a beautiful woman suffering a terminal illness and suffering it well. I would have been believable in the part of a tragic young woman at the end of her life. Had I really come that close? I didn't feel like I was dying, even though my heart ached. I felt painfully alive.

I slid my feet into some strappy sandals. I was confused and feeling sick from hunger. I had no idea how long Owen had held me. The days had blended together in a long taffy-like string of dawns and sunsets and nights. The walls of my cell seemed to press in on me. My chest tightened and I closed my eyes, a sudden moment of panic overtaking me. Then a long, lonely bird cry called out from outside my window. I forced myself to take a deep breath, and slowly opened my eyes. First, I looked out over the balcony, then let my gaze wander back through the room.

The clothes in the dresser caught my eye, and I stroked the ruined dress I had worn the night Owen had taken me to the mountain to have dinner. The last place I'd seen it was in tatters on the floor of his bedroom. I tore a piece of silk off the edge of the skirt and used it to tie my hair into a ponytail, then I left the rags where they were. I tossed the other clothes onto the bed and tied the corners of the sheet together to form a bundle. I went to the bathroom and tossed all the fine toiletries and make up into the cash bag. When I hoisted the cumbersome lump and walked toward the door, I felt like a kid running away to join the circus. It seemed petty to take these things with me, like a tourist stealing soaps from a hotel, but damned if I was going to leave it all there. Bag of cash aside, I felt more than entitled. I had no plan and no idea of how I was going to get out of there. I was just leaving. I had freedom, and I wasn't sure I still wanted it.

Well, I mean sure I did. I wanted my life back. But I didn't want my life back alone. I wanted Owen with me.

The doorknob would not turn for a moment my hands were so slippery with sweat, and I started to panic, but it finally did. I walked out the door. It was the first time I had not been carried or fled too fast down the hallway to appreciate the place, but

as soon as I got to the third door, I knew what was wrong with it. Only a few rooms were furnished. The rest of the house was unused and empty.

I wandered into the kitchen, trying to recall exactly where he had stood the first time I had opened my eyes to see him standing in the shadows. The wall showed a slight repair where he had manacled me that first day. Kneeling, I could see a small dark stain on one base board, a missed spot of my blood. There were still the remains of food in the fridge, bacon, eggs, spinach, and a number of different cheeses, cream, and what looked like a fish fillet wrapped in paper. I made myself breakfast, taking my time to leisurely explore the kitchen and eat. I was stalling, hoping he would come back. It felt weird, eating at a table I'm not sure had ever been sat at, looking out the picture window at the sea. I'd pulled back all the block-out curtains, filling the dim rooms with sunlight.

The silence echoed endlessly around me. I sighed and took one long breath, then another. I closed my eyes and waited in the red veined darkness, hoping to find one last trace of him, to smell his particular smell, or to hear a soft footfall, but there was nothing but the dry wind outside tapping lightly against the windows.

I found two rooms on the lowest floor. One had no furnishings, except a tiny nest of blankets curled into a corner that had a rank wild smell. A single tube of lipstick lay in the rags. This must have been Loretta's lair. The other was Owen's room. His wardrobe had been cleared out. No clothes left, no books. Owen was gone.

His smell lingered in one of the pillows though, and I clutched it to my chest.

"Come back, you cowardly bastard!" I screamed, but there was no answer. He had left me.

It was late afternoon when I decided I might as well go. Shouldering my hobo sack of clothing and sheets, I stomped out the front door, slamming it behind me.

In the driveway sat my car. I stared at it, disbelieving. It was mine all right, the same dinged fender and fading paint job. I put my hand on the hood, certain I was hallucinating, and the metal scorched my fingers. I yanked them back and stuck the burning tips in my mouth to cool them. I wondered for a moment how long it had been there. Had he been keeping it at the club or in a garage, or had it been there the entire time, just steps from the door? I couldn't recall seeing it on my last desperate bid for escape, but all I really remembered was blinding sunlight, and then the strength of Owen's arms around me, pulling me back.

My windows were open, the keys in the ignition. I really was free. I got in and cranked the engine, expecting to hear the usual nothing I got from the old and faulty battery when the car hadn't been started

for a while. It rumbled easily to life, running smoother than it used to. My purse was on the passenger seat, and beside it my cell phone blinked on. I stared at it, stopping there in the apex between the drive and the street. I'm not sure how the phone even still had battery. Had Owen charged it for me, too?

I lifted it up. Five messages, three from bill collectors, one from a girl I knew asking if I wanted to go out to a club that night, and one from my mom. The date showed me I had been with Owen for more than three weeks. Three weeks, and all I had were two personal messages. How sad. And to be honest, I knew the motives behind all of them. The girl was someone who liked to have a big entourage along wherever she went, and cared little who was in it. The message from my mom was just a guilt trip about not remembering to call on her birthday. I would have, if I hadn't been chained up by a vampire at the time. Tossing my phone back onto the passenger seat, I decided I would call her later. I really needed to concentrate more on people—real, living people—and forging friendships in the future.

Then maybe if I was abducted again for three weeks, someone would care.

I clicked on my navigator and headed back to the city.

My roommate and landlord, Lisa, stared at me as I walked in the door.

"Where the hell have you been? We were just about to toss your stuff into the living room and have a free-for-all with it."

Her eyes swept down my body, taking in the quality of my outfit, and I glared at her. Lisa was a clothes thief of the worst sort. She would wear other people's stuff and put it back reeking of cigarettes and beer and sweat, then swear she had never touched it. She had ruined more of my clothes than I could count. I'd taken to keeping my good clothes in the trunk of my car, because it was the only way I could keep them safe.

I gave her a level smile. "Oh, you know..." I waved

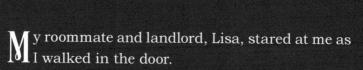

a hand in the air in a casual gesture. "I met this guy … He had this awesome motorcycle, and was headed down to Mexico for a few days …" I added a half-embarrassed titter. It was a pretty terrible lie, but I'm an actress. Making terrible lies believable is what I do.

She shrugged before answering, "Yeah, that happens. You got some shit bad bruises there. You guys take a spill?" She didn't bother getting up from the couch she was lounged across, smoke curling lazily from the cigarette between her fingers. The whole house reeked. There were dishes in the sink that were there from before I left, the walls were yellowed from smoke, and everything stank of pot and alcohol.

"You could say that. You know how it is, there's no fun unless it's dangerous." My tone was light but the words felt wooden. Her bird-bright eyes drifted to my wrist, then back to my face, a catty smirk saying she knew I'd been up to raunchy things.

"You have to pay your rent today, or I really will boot you out and keep your clothes." She got up, swaggering toward me. I stood my ground, though normally I would have ducked away and scurried to my room. I was done with that now.

I answered her with, "I'm moving out."

"You still owe from last month," she parried quickly. She thought I was leaving because I had a sugar daddy or something. I could tell from the way she eyed me. Lisa had never been able to keep her mouth shut or her nose out of other peoples' business.

I gave her a tight smile and handed her the four hundred bucks that was my share of the rent. She counted it, her slender and calloused fingers running across the bills expertly. "You still owe utilities."

"Take it out of the cost of all my clothes you fucked up," I said. I could feel a hardness surfacing in my eyes. She must have seen it too, because her tongue stilled, and she took a long step back. Normally she would have used sixty-seven swear words by now. I walked past her and grabbed my things, stuffing them into a couple of battered suitcases. I discovered my roommates had changed and that all of my stuff was in a box under a bathroom cabinet. Since I hadn't been there using my cupboard-room space they had rented it out to someone else. They all had just figured I had got a big gig and moved on or something. To see first-hand how little an impression I made on the world had opened my eyes in a big way. That was my life, or rather it had been. I had settled and half-stepped as long as I was going to. I had my life back, and damned if I was going to keep living it in half measures.

A tear crept out of my right eye and slid down my cheek. Owen had taught me to trust that even

if there was nothing below my feet, I could survive a fall. I was still afraid of what was going to happen next, of what might happen if I failed, but I wasn't going to let it keep me from doing it. I had to try.

I walked out with my head held high. I never looked back.

It was time for me to soar.

Harvey stared up at me, his moon like face registering first shock, then dismay, then a leer that made me want to shower immediately.

"Damn, Kitty, you look great! Did you get a facial, or your teeth professionally whitened, or something? Hey, I got your money from the LARP game here." He reached into his drawer and pulled out his check book, hastily scribbling one out. I took it from him. He didn't need to know Owen had paid me that and more. The jackass agent owed me.

I shoved the check into the pocket of my jeans, tapped a foot, and glared at him, "You mean I look great for someone you thought would be dead by now?"

His face went pale. "Aw c'mon, what's that supposed to mean?"

"You were the *only person* who knew where I was,

Harvey. Did you report me missing? Tell anyone? No, you were just damned glad one of your troublesome clients was gone. You send a lot of the porn girls out to those games, don't you? Or worse? How many never come back?" I slammed my hands down on his desk. "Don't try to be cute Harvey, I don't have any fucks left to give."

His lips twisted. I could see the wheels spinning in his head while he tried to think of something to say that would keep him out of trouble. "Always knew the games could get a bit rough, vampires have that whole snuff fantasy vibe. When you didn't come back, I kind of figured ... hey, it's not my fault all right? I'm just a guy trying to help new talent get a start in this town. I didn't want my name getting dragged into some investigation." He spread his thick hands out and gave me an insincere smile. The thing was, I knew he was telling a partial truth. He honestly didn't think it was his problem. He had no concern for the welfare of the girls he sent. I'm not sure he knew exactly the danger he'd sent them into, but he knew it was dangerous. I answered by spitting in his face.

He rocked backward in his chair, and his eyes narrowed down to slits. "That ain't nice, Kitty. You could get hurt playing like that." His voice lost some of its oily charm, a hint of a rougher tone creeping in as his composure slipped.

I saw his hand just then. He had a new ring. Black tarnished silver with a bloody tear-drop shaped ruby twinkling malevolently.

I blinked. Could the cursed ring be real? And did Harvey really deserve it? If the legend was true, then he did. Maybe he did a lot worse than sending porn stars to rough games. God knows what fates he's been sending girls to. Or could its appearance here have something to do with Owen?

I almost considered warning Harvey, but I'd just sound crazy if I tried. It made me pause though, and he started talking again. Like I really cared what he had to say.

"Kitty, Kitty. It's all water under the bridge anyway. You're here, you're fine, and I think I got a part for you," he said, leaning back in his chair so hard it creaked. He must have decided we were still friends after all. Of course, he believed I was there to see if he had any other work for me. He thought I still needed him. His arms lifted to reveal sweat stains under his pits. Large yellow tinted patches that made me curl my nose. Had I ever been so naïve as to think this guy had my best interests at heart? He shuffled through some of his papers and started telling me about some minor gig, the same D-list crap he'd always given me. I wasn't listening anymore.

"I'm getting a new agent, Harvey," I said, and walked out the door. "Enjoy your evening."

unLife

The door closed behind me, cutting off his retort, and I leaned against it. My heart was pounding, and a goofy grin creased my face. It had been an odd day, to say the least. I had left my prison, and left my home and roommates. And now, Harvey was dealt with.

I dusted my hands and headed out into the twilight. It felt like starting over, a fresh new try at life. Owen might not have bled me dry, but he had killed the old me. I was still getting to know the new one. I think I liked her. As I was getting into my car, I saw a thick clot of shadows gathering around the doorway to Harvey's office. I stared at them in horror, remorse filling me. Then I cranked my engine. Harvey would face the ones he hurt, as we all do eventually. I had not brought that on him, he had done it to himself.

19

It only took a week for me to make the decision to go to Owen's club to try to see him. The façade was boarded up, under renovations. The large chrome letters reading *Dark Raine* were being taken down, replaced with a new neon sign. A banner pasted across the front of the boarding said, "Under New Management. Re-Opening Soon."

I went into full-on stalker mode. I hunted down any information about Owen Raine I could find online. There were a few basic entries about his business life, and one new article which did little more than say the reclusive businessman had recently become more reclusive. There was nothing in public records revealing what property he owned. It was though he hardly existed at all—just a ghost passing through. I spent a whole weekend pouring through the vast archives of the internet, filing away any snippet I could find. And I eventually found more. I dug further back, collecting scans of old articles, obituaries, anything where his name was mentioned. There were small notices from old newspapers announcing the business being passed on to a 'son' or other male heir, and an obituary for the old man saying that he had died quietly at home in the company of his only family. Owen, trading in one identity for another, father to son, as he lived through the centuries. It wasn't much to go on, but I obsessed over every scrap. Even though I was the only one who used my laptop, I hid it all in a folder called 'whatever' and pretended it didn't exist unless I was putting something in it.

I told myself to get over it, to forget him, move on, and consider myself lucky he was gone. But I couldn't. God, I missed him so much I thought my chest would implode. Every night as sunset fell, I waited for him, expecting him to walk into my life again. Maybe I just needed counseling, but it felt like more than that. Besides, what would I say? Hi, my name's Kitty, I fell in love with a vampire who kept me prisoner because he loved the taste of my blood? Fat chance. I hadn't known love before, but if this wasn't what it felt like, I don't know what it would.

Nights stretched long and lonely, and I had trouble

sleeping. I took to swimming in the pool of my new complex. It kept me fit at least, even if it didn't keep the dark circles at bay. I missed the smell of roses and jasmine.

I drove by Owen's house every day. It was always empty and abandoned. It had begun to take on a sort of derelict appearance by the time I saw a man outside of it. I pulled into the drive, eager to find out what was going on. He came to meet me, his eyes taking in my crappy car with something like dismay.

"Hey there, Walter Longbow," he said, reaching out a friendly hand.

"Kaitlyn French."

"Are you here for the house sale?"

"I'm sorry, I wasn't aware it was on the market."

"Oh well, it's still a private listing," he hastened to add, his face saying he doubted I was there to buy.

The house was being sold. Another tie to Owen severed. "I was actually here to see Owen."

"You know Mister Raine?"

"Sort of. I don't suppose you know where I could find him?"

Walter shook his head and raised an eyebrow skeptically. "I wouldn't be able to share his private address, even if I could."

I tried to laugh casually and not seem like a stalker. "Oh no, I didn't mean like that. I meant right now, like, if he was just around the back or something."

"No. I only deal with Mister Raine by email. I handle a few of his properties for him, and to be honest, I was surprised he decided to sell this one. It's been in his family a long time." Walter loosened up. "You know Mister Raine's great-grandfather built this house in the nineteen-twenties. He was a heavy player during the prohibition, then one day, he just retired. He retreated to this house and shunned everyone. Nobody knew why."

Because he was not aging would have been my guess as to why he'd retreated from the world. Because the isolation suited him. Because he had grown weary of trying to fit into a world in which he did not feel he belonged. I said none of those things. I could only guess, and know that all of them were partly true. And there were probably a dozen other reasons I couldn't fathom.

"Anyway, he left it to his son, who left it to his son, not that they ever came here, except on the rarest of occasions. The house was only used a few months of every year, which seems a shame given it's so lovely. But Mister Raine has properties all over the country, and abroad. This one was renovated just last year. It was a bit in need of it, but he took care to make sure the original character of the place remained. I understand he did much of the work himself, and he takes as much pride in his work as the man who built it."

unLife

He is the man who built it, and he could be anywhere. Anywhere in the world.

I stared at the mansion, using it as a distraction while I fought to hold back tears. It was lovely, in a stark and forbidding way. I wondered, briefly, if the tennis court was still stained where Loretta had fallen. I had never dared look down to see what he had done with it. I tried my best not to think about it at all really. "It is an amazing house."

Walter touched one hand to his too-perfect-to-be-anything-other-than-fake hair. "Since you're here, would you like to look at the inside of the home?" He was putting on his best realtor face. I assumed it was habit for him, just like it was habit for me to pretend that Owen didn't exist, despite the fact that I looked for him in every brown-haired stranger.

"I've seen it. I lived here for a short time."

Walter perked up, leaning toward me conspiratorially. "Is it really haunted like they say?"

"Not anymore," I said, and climbed back into my car. I gave the house one last look, because I knew I would never come back. There was no longer any need to. All hopes I had that Owen would return had been dashed by a real estate agent in a toupee and off-the-rack suit. Dreams get killed by the most mundane of things sometimes.

20

S ix months later, I was walking in a farmer's market, basking in the smell of flowers, and freshly baked bread, and a last few moments of anonymity.

It had been a hell of a time for me in many ways, both good and bad. I had marched into the office of Jenny Kurtz, the best agent around, darting past her security and secretary like a ninja. I made it into her office, where she was talking with a well-known director.

I looked at them both and said, "I'm Kaitlyn French. I'm your newest client. You may not remember taking me on, because you haven't yet. But I know you will."

Jenny had laughed out loud. The intense little man sitting in the chair across Jenny's rosewood

SELINA A. FENECH

desk had asked me to stand in the bright sunlight coming from the windows. I had, and he had gotten very close to my face, surveying it like it was a work of art and he was looking for minute cracks. Then he handed me a script and asked me to read a few lines with him.

I did. The part called for me to be angry, and I was plenty that. It called for me to be hurting, and I damn sure was. It was a role made for me. When I'd finished reading the few lines he'd asked for, I was shaking from adrenaline and emotion. The looks they gave me had been cautious, like they weren't sure if I was crazy or not. So, I pushed all my feelings into a little box, and put on my best, winning actress smile. The director handed me his card. Jenny shook my hand and told her secretary to get the necessary paperwork.

The very next day, I was screen testing for that role. They wanted to see how I looked on film, and lo and behold I got the part. It was a supporting role, but a major one, in a major film. It would be released in cinemas worldwide tomorrow.

Filming had been exhausting. Because of the time crunch, I had been on set pretty much non-stop. In the beginning of the movie, I had just played a bitchy goth girl. Easy enough. It was the end that had been hard, playing too close a parallel to my real life. The screenplay had my character falling in love, as it turned out, with the villain of the story. She disappeared for half the movie, and when the main female and male leads found her again, she'd been used and abused, imprisoned, and driven insane so that she believed she was still in love with the man who had hurt her. The director praised the complexity I brought to the role, the character's struggle to know what she really wanted or needed. *Yeah, I wonder where I pulled that from?*

It had only taken a few takes to get it down, and for that I was grateful. I wasn't sure I could do it again without breaking apart completely in front of the whole cast and crew.

I'd kept to myself for a while after filming ended, but now I was finally starting to feel better. I was starting to feel more myself, and damn if I wasn't excited for the premier. That, and Jenny had me working hard. The work kept me from dwelling on my past too long. From dwelling on Owen, and the hole he'd left in me.

Things were good. I had a brand new agent, one of the best who was determined to push me to new heights. I had just finished filming four television appearances, and Jenny was already negotiating my role in three new films. More than that, I liked her. She seemed like a genuinely good person. She'd called me up once or twice when filming was over, asking how I was doing and checking if I was ready for more work. I never had to ask, as long as I said I could take it she always had work for me. And I wanted the work. I wanted to be busy. I was living more comfortably than I had in a long time. I still hadn't told my parents that I thought I was going somewhere. I didn't want them to say 'I told you so' if I failed. Still, I was making the effort to call them, and to mend some of the relationships I'd ruined when I left home.

Harvey, on the other hand, was found dead in his office. The coroner ruled it a massive heart attack, which could easily have been true. Whether it was really caused by a cursed ring was something I tried not to think about. Some things you can't explain or find logical little boxes for. Some things you don't want to have to answer. Or answer for.

Life was mostly normal though. I still jumped at shadows, but I hadn't seen anything supernatural since my release. I sometimes felt like I was being followed, particularly at night. I often thought I saw people who looked like they didn't belong in this world, but to be honest, it's hard to tell in Hollywood. I don't ever try to get close enough to look in their eyes. I'd started to see all kinds of things in the dark, now that I knew vampires were real. That meant anything was possible. It was enough to make me jumpy after dusk, and sometimes kept me awake at night. Not that I could sleep anyway. I was always too busy waiting for the night to bring Owen back to me.

I still have a scar on my throat.

"Strawberry?"

The single word knocked me from my reverie. I turned back to see a grocer holding up a tray of strawberries to sample. "Try one. Best you've ever tasted. Get two punnets for the price of one."

The man standing in the stall held out the plump and juicy fruit. I stared at it, my heart aching. He called again to another passerby, and my eyes closed, remembering the way that word had fallen from Owen's lips.

Had anything ever been as sweet as that? In all that had changed in my life, in all the good I'd found, I still missed him. My eyes opened to see the stallholder looking at me carefully. He held out the sun-warmed fruit. "Here, try it."

I placed the ripened berry between my lips. It broke open between my teeth. Juice spilled across my tongue, filled my mouth, and tears hung in my eyes.

"It's so sweet." I licked the juice from my lips, savoring the flavor.

But I wasn't going to buy from him, not today. Maybe tomorrow I'd return and pick up enough to make something divine. Or perhaps I'd just eat them as they were, while I read a book in the bay window.

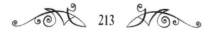

Truth was though, I just couldn't eat strawberries anymore without crying my eyes out, wishing Owen would come back to me.

I turned away quickly so I could wipe my eyes, and I caught sight of a familiar face, staring at me through the aisle between stalls. My heart stuttered to a standstill.

I'd had false sightings too many times before. Owen haunted my dreams, and my waking life, too. I thought I saw him everywhere, but when I chased him down it would be some perfectly ordinary guy looking back at me. One of them had asked me out, one had given me a look that said I was nuts, and one had been so startled he had dropped his bag of groceries.

The man turned away in an instant and headed off through the market. It was broad daylight. I knew it couldn't be him, but I had to follow him anyway.

His hair was a lighter shade than I remembered Owen's being, and shorter. He was muscular without being bulky and moved with a lithe grace. It was the way he moved that inflamed a tiny bit of hope in me, and impossible desire. Owen had always moved with such precision. He was never clumsy or out of sorts. The set of his shoulders, and length of his strides, just seemed too familiar. He wore a grey shirt rolled up to the elbows that showed his lightly tanned arms off to perfection. Tanned? It wasn't him. It couldn't be. There was no forgetting the pallor of Owen's skin.

I almost left it at that, when the man turned his face around quickly to check behind him, meeting my gaze.

It *was* him. My heart clenched like a fist then bloomed back open. My head spun. *It was him!* There was no mistaking it, no mistaking those lips or the high angles of his cheeks. Even from a distance, I could see the blue of his eyes. I remembered how they had faded away from black to periwinkle. It was him, of that there was absolutely no doubt. He was as magnificent a man as ...

He was *human*. That thought hit me and staggered me. That was what his grabbing his chest had been all about, his heart had begun to beat again for the first time in centuries! My blood had restored him to his human form, and what had I gotten in return for that? Ten grand, a new wardrobe, and abandoned like a one night stand? I have lousy taste in guys. I should have known he would be no better than the rest of them. Anger suddenly ripped through my heart. It didn't override my desire for him, it just made me want to smack him as much as I wanted to kiss him. And I really wanted to kiss him.

Why was he here? It had looked as though he had been following me, but as soon as I spotted him, he had turned away. Had he been keeping

tabs on me? Was it possible he missed me as much as I missed him?

He was walking away faster than before, his arms swinging by his sides. I couldn't hesitate, because if I did, I would lose sight of him, perhaps forever.

I pushed through the crowd, throwing apologies over my shoulder to those I bumped. He crossed the hot parking lot and I ran after him, my heart beating so hard and fast I was sure I was going to topple to the ground.

I wet my lips with my tongue and called out. "Owen!"

He kept walking. My heart plummeted. I caught up and grabbed his arm. He swung around to look at me, his face carefully blank and his eyes inscrutable. I faltered a little, but I knew it was him. Unless he had some progeny he'd never told me about that was his spitting image in human form …

"Can I help you, Miss?"

"It's me." I ran my gaze over his face, the face I had once hated to see and had missed so much since it had been gone from my sight. "It's me, Kitty."

"I'm sorry. I think you have me mixed up with someone else." He withdrew his arm gently.

"The hell I do. I know it's you, stop pretending it isn't."

"I'm not who you think I am." His voice held an aching tenderness. His eyes were kind and warm, but there was hurt underneath, I could see it. Why was he hurt? He wasn't allowed to be hurt when he was the one who left me! I was hurting too, dammit. Couldn't he see that? Didn't he care?

Tears as corrosive as battery acid sprang to my eyes, and my throat filled with a salty lump that would not let me speak, let alone refute his words. I had been mistaken before, but not this time. I knew him, knew him all too well.

He turned away, reaching for his keys. I heard the locks on the sleek black sports car disengage, and I knew this was my only chance. If I let him drive away from me, he would likely leave LA and my chances of ever finding him again were slim to none.

I said, so low that I knew those around us couldn't hear but he could, "Don't you turn away from me. Face me, dammit. You owe me that, Vampire."

His shoulders slumped and he turned toward me. Guilt creased his features, and he met my eyes. "Strawberry," he sighed. "You always were too persistent."

I fell onto his chest, swallowing away the sob that rose in mine. The solid warmth of his body met me like a wall, and I welcomed it. He was real, he was there, and I hugged him so tightly I could hear his back creaking. The warmth of him was what really struck me. Every time I had touched him before I had expected it, only to find his skin cold and

inhuman. Now, it was hot, sunbaked. I could even smell a faint whiff of sweat and leather, probably from the car seats. Good smells, living smells.

"It really is you," I said. "And you're really human?"

He stiffened in my arms but I held on, not letting go. Like hell I was going to let him go again.

He breathed out a long sigh. "Yes. Something in your amazing blood transformed me. I had felt the change coming, the slow progression of my humanity coming back to me, but almost didn't believe it until that morning after we made love. I walked into the daylight, and I did not burn. You made my heart beat again, and you gave it something to beat for."

I looked up into his eyes. "Then why did you leave me?"

"When I found myself human, I also found that I had fallen in love with you. In that moment, I realized the tragedy that had befallen me. How could you ever forgive me for what I'd done to you? How could you, when I could never forgive myself? I had kept you, against your will." He looked truly horrified at the memory. He turned away and wouldn't meet my eyes, but for that moment it didn't matter. I rested my cheek against his chest, listening to the soft, steady thump of his heart.

"You ... fell in love with me?" Trust a girl to focus on that part.

"Heart, body, and soul." His voice was barely a

whisper, like his confession pained him, stealing his breath. "But I knew you could never love me in return after the crimes I had committed against you. I had done you such wrong ... I had to let you be free of me. I had to leave."

"You were a monster," I said. He flinched and looked away again. I reached a hand to his chin and turned him back to face me. "*Were* a monster. I love the man who was trapped within. I love Owen Raine, not the vampire that possessed you for so long. You are human again, and it doesn't matter what the cost was. I don't love the monster that imprisoned me. I love the man who set me free."

He held me, crushing me to him as though afraid I'd disappear. My face pressed into his chest and I could hear it, his heart, drumming a steady beat. I loved the sound. Closing my eyes, a hundred days and nights seemed to flick before my eyes, falling asleep bathed in moonlight to the sound, and waking up to the brilliant morning sun with it still steadily beating by my ear. I picked up one of his hands and held it to the sun, the sunlight turned it red, outlining the veins below his skin.

He smelled of cologne, something subtle and expensive, but the coppery scent of blood had left him. He was a human, a man, and the one I wanted to love forever, for the rest of our natural lives.

"What are you even doing here? I mean, why? Why

have I found you again now?" I asked, breathlessly.

"Can I make a confession?" Owen said softly.

"Confess away."

Owen's eyes darkened with concern. "I've been keeping an eye on you. I'm sorry, I know that's not the done thing these days, and I don't want to seem strange, or overprotective, or possessive. I had reason to be worried about you. If your blood was at all as appealing to other vampires as it was to me, I considered you could be at great risk if you ever crossed a vampire's path again."

"I suppose that makes sense," I rolled the words slowly off my tongue. I had often wondered the same thing. It made me feel special, and safe, to know Owen had been worried about me. "Except that no vamp is going to steal me away from a daylight market, now are they?"

Owen grinned bashfully. "Mostly I've had some men I hired keep you under surveillance. But when one reported some suspicious activity, I had to come myself. I needed to know, after all you'd suffered, I just needed to know you were okay. I needed to see you. Perhaps the more honest truth was that I just could never let my Strawberry go, as much as I knew I should.

"I'm sorry. I didn't want you to see me, too," he said, pressing his lips into my hair. I could feel the warm trickle of a tear on my face but it was not mine, it was his. "I did not know how to handle the emotions that came with being human again. I did not know how to be a good man, maybe I never did. Your blood changed me, made me something far better, and I can't believe you would ever be able to look at me and not see the vampire that had harmed you."

I leaned back to look at him. He seemed confused, and I felt a mischievous smile steal across my face. I stepped away, feeling his hands clutch at me for a moment before reluctantly giving way and allowing me to move freely.

"What if we just start over?" I held out my hand to shake his. "I'm Kaitlyn, Kaitlyn French. I'm an actress, and I'm not doing too badly at it. I like food, especially good food, castles, and happy endings."

He smiled a lop-sided smile that sent arrows of lust slicing into my heart. "I'm Owen Raine. I'm a multimillionaire businessman who currently lives on a ranch with horses. I like grocery shopping, because every time I go, there is some new and wonderful food to try. I just learned how to use a computer in order to keep up with the world better. I googled you, just so you know. I recently began to 'hang out' on the beach, and I have learned to like dining in restaurants."

"It's nice to meet you," I said, shaking his hand, both of us laughing.

He twined his fingers through mine. His smile was full of the boyish ruefulness I'd only seen once before, and I cherished it. In the touch of his fingers, his skin hot against mine, and the way his blue eyes saw into me, I knew that he felt the same way about me as I did about him. He'd said it, sure, but neither of us were the best with words. Our souls resonated with each other though, proving the truth in both our hearts.

The day shone down on us as he pulled me in for a slow, tender kiss. I wanted to keep that moment forever, but knew I didn't have to. I had Owen again, and he loved me, and I loved him, and everything was right in my life.

Never before had I felt so loved.

Now and forever, I belonged to him.

His strawberry.

He whispered in my ear, "I'm glad you're going by Kaitlyn French now. I like it. Sounds less like a porn star."

"Oh, bite me."

How long can Kaitlyn and Owen live their
happily ever after before another vampire
discovers her tempting blood?

FIND OUT IN

HeartsBlood

BOOK TWO

Remortality

ABOUT THE AUTHOR

Whether it's painting artworks or writing novels, creating fantasy works is Selina's biggest passion. She lives in Australia with her husband and daughter and loves food, gardening, geekery, and all things fantasy.

FIND OUT MORE ABOUT SELINA

Official Website www.selinafenech.com

MORE BOOKS BY
SELINA A. FENECH

CPSIA information can be obtained
at www.ICGtesting.com
Printed in the USA
BVHW062023011221
622865BV00006B/171

9 781922 390271